Freshman Frenzy

Books by Beverly Lewis

GIRLS ONLY (GO!)
Youth Fiction

Dreams on Ice	*Follow the Dream*
Only the Best	*Better Than Best*
A Perfect Match	*Photo Perfect*
Reach for the Stars	*Star Status*

SUMMERHILL SECRETS
Youth Fiction

Whispers Down the Lane	*House of Secrets*
Secret in the Willows	*Echoes in the Wind*
Catch a Falling Star	*Hide Behind the Moon*
Night of the Fireflies	*Windows on the Hill*
A Cry in the Dark	*Shadows Beyond the Gate*

HOLLY'S HEART
Youth Fiction

Best Friend, Worst Enemy	*Good-Bye, Dressel Hills*
Secret Summer Dreams	*Straight-A Teacher*
Sealed With a Kiss	*No Guys Pact*
The Trouble With Weddings	*Little White Lies*
California Crazy	*Freshman Frenzy*
Second-Best Friend	*Mystery Letters*

www.BeverlyLewis.com

Freshman Frenzy

Beverly Lewis

BETHANYHOUSE
Minneapolis, Minnesota

Freshman Frenzy
Copyright © 2003
Beverly Lewis

Cover design by Cheryl Neisen

Published by Bethany House Publishers
11400 Hampshire Avenue South
Bloomington, Minnesota 55438
www.bethanyhouse.com

Bethany House Publishers is a Division of
Baker Book House Company, Grand Rapids, Michigan.

Printed in the United States of America

Library of Congress Cataloging-in-Publication Data

Lewis, Beverly, 1949–
    Freshman Frenzy / by Beverly Lewis. — [Rev.,updated ed.]
        p.   cm. — (Holly's heart ; 11)
Summary: When the ninth graders are suddenly moved from the overcrowded
junior high to become the new high school freshman class, Holly and her
lifelong best friend Andie have some trouble finding their rightful places.
    ISBN 0-7642-2618-5 (pbk.)
    [1. High schools—Fiction. 2. Schools—Fiction. 3. Friendship—Fiction.
4. Christian life—Fiction.] I. Title. II. Series: Lewis, Beverly, 1949-   .
Holly's heart series ; 11.

PZ7.L58464Fj   2003
[Fic]—dc21
                                                                    2003001426

Author's Note

It's exciting for me, the creator of Holly-Heart, to see my character growing up . . . now a freshman in high school! I love the way my readers have supported and encouraged me to continue writing this series. Many of you have prayed for me, sent favorite Scripture verses, and made lovely cards or sent e-notes pleading for more books. How delighted I am that you are getting your wish— more of the HOLLY'S HEART series.

A big thank-you to my wonderful kid consultant group: Shanna, Larissa, Mindie, Janie, Julie, Brandy, Amy, and Jon.

And what would I do without my cool husband, Dave? Watching him pore over the manuscript, even though I keep telling him it's for *girls*, is fabulous fun! Anyway, what a big help he is, editorially speaking and otherwise!

For my cool niece
Amy Birch.
Happy freshman year!

And . . .
For a very special fan
in Roseville, MN—
Beth Alexander.

My freshman year was doomed, thanks to the Dressel Hills, Colorado, school board.

"How can they do this?" I wailed, watching Mom prepare a casserole for supper.

"Well, try looking on the bright side." She offered a comforting smile. "You get to go to high school a whole year early."

"That's exactly the problem!" I argued.

She continued. "And don't forget, now you can see your tenth-grade friends every day."

That's cool, I thought. Friends like Danny Myers . . . and Stan Patterson, my brousin—cousin-turned-stepbrother.

I could almost see it now, Stan sneering down his sophomore nose at me. Probably all year long, too! I couldn't wait *not* to go.

Of course, my twin girl friends, Paula and Kayla Miller, would be there. An encouraging thought. But in spite of the togetherness aspect, it didn't change the fact that I was being cheated out of my last, fabulous year of junior high. Top of the heap was an honor. Something to look forward to. Something to remember . . . forever.

Lofty freshmen had always ruled the corridors of Dressel Hills Junior High. Paula and Kayla were constantly talking about how cool it was last year. Now, just when it was my turn to be in the highest class on campus, I was being shoved out—off to high school, returning to the bottom of the barrel.

I stared at Mom's creamy chicken-and-rice casserole.

It smelled perfectly delicious, even with the broccoli bits not-so-subtly mixed in. But my appetite had vanished. How could the voting public possibly think this was a good move? So what if the junior high was too crowded? I mean, come on—it was a rip-off for us freshmen. Didn't we deserve our rightful privilege?

I must've sighed or something. Anyway, Mom glanced at me. "You're taking this too hard, Holly-Heart."

"I don't know how else to take it, Mom! I just can't deal with it. It's just so . . . so . . ."

The sparkle faded from her cheerful eyes. "What?"

"It's so unfair!" I blurted.

"Life's not always fair. You and I both know that." She turned around to set the oven timer.

I shrugged and headed upstairs to my room. Mom was too glib. Sure, she'd been through her teen years and lived to tell about it—eons ago.

How could she possibly remember how it felt to be my age?

I hurried upstairs to my desk. I owed someone a letter. A very special someone—sixteen-year-old Sean Hamilton. The boy I'd met last Christmas while visiting my dad in California. Sean was the sweetest guy I'd ever met. Best of all, he was a Christian.

I'd surprised myself and faithfully answered each of his letters since returning home five weeks ago. In fact, my correspondence with Sean was getting to be very interesting. His letters were friendly enough; he was open about his life goals and other things.

I reached for a box of pastel pink stationery and picked up my pen.

Thursday, August 29
(Four days of freedom before school starts!)
Dear Sean,

Hey. How's everything out there? Did you get your car fixed? If not, are you still jogging to your summer job at the radio station?

I guess there's not really much to write about. I mean, there is—it's just that I'm not sure if you'd be that interested. Okay! I can hear you saying, "Go ahead and tell me."

Well, to begin with, the schools here are over-crowded, and sixth graders are being required to move up to middle school. That pushes the freshmen (me) up to high school. And, you guessed it, I'll have to deal with initiation and stuff. Worse than that, I'm going to miss being top dog in junior high. Being on the low end of the totem pole doesn't sound like much fun. But, oh well, I guess I'll survive. I have no choice, right?

School starts next Tuesday.

I was wondering, did you have to go through high-school initiation as a freshman? If you did, what kinds of things did they do to you? I'm dying to know, so I can prepare myself. Ha!

Actually, it's not very funny. When I think about it, sometimes I feel like crying. That might sound dumb to you, but it's true.

Anyway, life stinks here.

Hope your school year's better than mine!

Your friend,
Holly

I reread the letter and decided it sounded almost too personal, especially the crying part. I thought about rewriting the whole thing. Then I got the idea to dig out Sean's letters to see how he'd expressed some of the concerns about his life.

After looking through them, I decided to let my words stand as written and sealed the envelope. Personal or not, Sean would be reading it in about three days. Mom hadn't understood my feelings about school. I hoped Sean Hamilton would.

2

After supper I walked to the mailbox to mail my letter. Since it was still light out—and I wanted to avoid another conversation at home—I continued walking down the brick sidewalk.

The sky was full of small, shredded clouds floating across deep-blue space. Summer was winding down in more ways than one. Everywhere I looked, families on Downhill Court—my street—were outdoors grilling hamburgers. The final relaxed moments of summer would soon dissolve into hectic hustle of kids bustling back to school.

Three blocks down, I came to Aspen Street, the only stretch of road leading into and out of town. Compared to the bumper-to-bumper traffic during ski season, the street seemed long now.

A musty, nostalgic feeling swept the air—a hint of fall, I guess—accompanied by an unexpected breeze. I shivered a bit. The minute the sun set in Dressel Hills, things began to cool off. Even in late August.

Colorado mountain towns are like that. After all, we aren't far from the continental divide. Top of the world.

Just not top of the heap.

I sighed, thinking about my old junior high. And the lost ninth-grade, top-dog status. Gone forever! The more I thought about it, the more frustrating it seemed.

Then, just as I was about to explode, I noticed my best friend, Andrea Martinez, coming out of the doughnut shop. She wore her church camp T-shirt and faded blue jean shorts. Her hair framed her face in dark curls. "Hey, Andie!" I called.

"Hey!" She waved back.

I had to know what she thought about the school mess. "Heard the latest?"

"Unfortunately." She wrinkled up her nose. "What's going to happen to us lowly freshmen?"

"That's what I'm worried about." I began to tell her how I'd flung my concerns on my mom.

Andie nodded. "My mom thinks it's too soon—moving us to high school a year early. She thinks I could stay in junior high another year. But honestly, she's a helicopter mom, you know, always hovering."

Andie's mother was more than overly protective. She was an outright worrywart.

"What they should do is give us freshmen our own wing of the school or something. Then we'd have something to claim and rule."

"Yeah," I agreed, "but who's going to suggest something like that?"

Andie fluffed her curly locks. "I will."

"Excuse me?"

"You're looking at the president-to-be of the Dressel Hills High freshman class!"

"Don't you wish." I studied her, waiting for the usual hilarious outburst. But she was confident, smiling. "When did you decide this?"

"Oh, a bunch of us were talking at the Soda Straw a little while ago."

"Today?" A strange, left-out feeling poked at me.

"Uh-huh." She glanced at me. I could tell by the recognition in her eyes she'd caught on. She knew how lousy I was feeling. Growing up as someone's best friend tends to give instant insight to the other person's feelings. "Aw, c'mon, it's not like we planned a meeting or anything," she said, obviously trying to back away from the subject. "It just happened."

"So . . . who all was there?"

"Just people."

"Right." Now her private little planning party had been reduced to "people." I stared at her bag of doughnuts. "What's going on?"

"Honestly, nothing. Paula and Kayla Miller were there having sundaes with Billy Hill and Danny Myers. All of us were kicking around some ideas."

I was all ears. "And?"

"Someone said I ought to run for freshman class president . . . that I'd make a good one, you know, a strong Christian voice in the school and on the student council." She grinned.

I agreed on *one* thing: Andie had a strong voice.

She continued. "Then Jared Wilkins and Amy-Liz Thompson showed up. When they heard what we were discussing, Jared came up with the idea that a bunch of us from church ought to think about running for student offices—we could evangelize the school."

I nodded, listening to her explain, although somewhat distracted. Jared and Amy-Liz— together?

Andie kept talking, but I tuned her out. It was easy to see she was off on one of her fantasy tangents. No way could she get voted in. Shoot, I hated to think this about my best friend, but there were lots of other, more popular, kids who stood a way better chance.

"Earth to Holly?"

I snapped out of it. "Huh?"

"Well, what do you think?"

I was still half dazed. "About what?"

"Will you be my campaign manager?"

Andie was serious about this running for president thing. I could see it in her eyes. "Uh . . . well, I guess I could. But, hey, wait a minute, how do you know I don't want to run?" I faked a good laugh. "I just might, you know."

"Oh, Holly," she groaned. "Give me a chance—just this once?"

I waited for her to stop whining. "Look, you don't have to worry. I'm going to be too busy adjusting to high school. You know how I am about my grades," I assured her.

"Yeah, you actually study!" she snickered.

"Just give me a year to settle in," I said. "Then watch out!"

Andie's eyes danced. "So you promise not to run?"

I nodded. "I really couldn't care less about all this. If you want to run, I'll manage your campaign."

She grabbed my arm and squeezed. "Oh, thank you! You won't be sorry, I promise!"

"What a relief," I teased, pulling the doughnut bag out of her hand. She chased me all the way to Downhill Court. We stopped running and started giggling in front of my next-door neighbor's house.

Mrs. Hibbard was entertaining her sewing-circle friends on the front porch. "Hello, girls," the elderly woman called to us.

Andie and I waved politely. "How are you doing, Mrs. Hibbard?" I replied.

"Oh, not too bad," she answered. "Won't you girls come join us for pie?" The thoughtful woman stood up and leaned on the porch banister. "Holly?" she called again without waiting for my reply.

I wanted to say no, but out of respect—and it was obvious she wanted us to come—we climbed the steps leading to her porch. "Hello," Andie and I greeted all her lady friends.

"Now, you just have a seat, girlies," Mrs. Hibbard said, hobbling off to get some pie. Soon she was back with an enormous piece of apple pie a la mode for both of us. "Here we are."

"Thank you," I said, conscious of five wrinkly faces staring at us. How long had it been since these senior citizens laid eyes on teen girls? Decades? Maybe longer? It sure felt that way, having five sets of eyes bore into our every move.

I slid my fork into the pie and tasted the fabulous dessert. "Mmm! Delicious," I said as they observed.

"Would you care for some tea?" one of them asked, leaning forward.

"No, thank you." I glanced over at Mrs. Hibbard and noticed that her eyes were transfixed on my hair. Reaching up, I felt the top of my head. Nothing unusual.

Mrs. Hibbard kept staring. "Your hair is so long and pretty, Holly," she said. "I remember seeing you as a wee girl, your hair flying free in the wind or gathered into a ponytail. Just the way you have it now."

Hearing her mention my childhood and associating it with my long hair made me feel uneasy. Here I was, on the verge of high school, wearing my hair the same old way. Maybe it was time for a change.

"Well, I've thought about doing something different with it. But the urge to change it comes and goes." I almost told her about going with my step-mom to an exclusive beauty salon in Beverly Hills while I visited in California last month. Saundra had nearly convinced me to have a spiral-wrap perm. She thought the crisp, vertical waves would look good with long, thick hair like mine. Daddy said so, too. But at the last minute I'd chickened out.

Mrs. Hibbard frowned a bit. "Don't you like your hair, Holly?"

"Oh, it's okay, I guess. I'm a little bored with it."

One of the other ladies chimed in. "I used to wear my hair down to my waist, too. But it got to be so heavy . . . bothered my neck."

"Well," I said, "I haven't had that problem. Not yet, anyway."

By now Andie was grinning like a Cheshire cat. For years she'd tried to get me to whack off my waist-length locks.

Mrs. Hibbard spoke up. "Well, my goodness, why would you want to cut your hair?"

I hadn't said anything about cutting it. Thoughtfully, I balanced my fork on my plate. "I'm not thinking of getting it cut—just permed."

"Oh, some curls," one of them said, flopping her hand forward in midair. "Well, why didn't you say so?"

I took another bite of pie.

Soon all of them were twittering about the pros and cons of perming. That's when Mrs. Hibbard offered to perm my hair for me. "I do my sister's hair all the time," she boasted. "There's nothing to it, really."

Gulp! The innocent look on her face frightened me. How could I get out of this gracefully?

I looked at Andie for moral support, but she was laughing so hard she nearly choked on her pie!

3

Without the slightest help from Andie, I salvaged Mrs. Hibbard's dignity and said thanks (but no thanks!) for offering to perm my hair.

"Close call," I said as Andie and I hurried across the lawn to my house.

"No kidding." She eyed me. "Don't tell me. This hair thing, it's about high school, right?"

Andie was like that—thought she knew what I was thinking before I ever said it. "Well, maybe," I said. "But it's time for a new look."

"So, what're you going to *do* with your new do?"

I giggled. "Ever hear of a spiral wrap?"

"Oh, no! Not that!" She clutched her throat.

"Come on, Andie—it'll be fine, you'll see."

"Your hair's way too long for that," she insisted. "It'll fry!"

The thought of that wiped me out. Who'd want to go to high school looking like a surge of electricity? "Are you sure?" I asked.

"C'mon, Holly. Perms can do that."

"What about conditioners and moisturizers— stuff like that?" No way was I ready to dismiss this perm business because of Andie's scare tactics.

"Fine," she huffed. "Go ahead; be a frizzy freshman. Just don't say I didn't warn you."

"Whatever," I muttered.

When Andie left I called to make an appointment with my mom's hairdresser. Unfortunately she was booked solid all day. Tomorrow, too. I was stuck. What could I do?

"I might be able to squeeze you in on Monday," the hairdresser said.

"You're working on Labor Day?" I asked.

The woman chuckled. "It's Labor Day. Somebody has to work."

So I agreed to have my hair done on Monday. One day before the first day of school. I must've been crazy to chance it like this. Andie's words rang in my ears. And I worried. What if my hair did frizz?

♥ ♥ ♥

I sat in the swivel salon chair, gazing at the plain, wide mirror in front of me. Family snapshots were scattered around the edges. Strange as it seemed, not one of the people in those pictures had a single curl!

I reached for my purse and found my brush. Last chance to whisk through my hair. Long, sweeping strokes. The silky feel, the length . . . it was all I'd ever known. Was I doing the right thing?

When my shampoo was finished, I spoke up. "My hair's never been permed before," I said. "In fact, except for the times you've trimmed it, it's never been cut."

The chubby woman smiled reassuringly. "Are you having second thoughts, hon?"

"Uh . . . sorta."

"Well, I could shorten the time for the perming solution." She rolled up her sleeves.

"Will that help?" I asked, feeling more and more unsure of myself.

"You seem worried."

I told her what Andie had said, and she promised to keep a close eye on things. Carefully, she sectioned off my hair and began to wrap the ends of my hair around each curler. It took over an hour to roll all my hair—one skinny strand at a time.

While I waited for the solution to do its thing, I read my new Marty Leigh mystery. I kept glancing up from my book, wondering what time it was. Listening for the timer . . . looking for Mom's spunky hairdresser.

I guess when you worry, you set yourself up for the very thing you fear to happen. Anyway, my hair frizzed up big time, exactly the way Andie said it would!

The hairdresser tried to smooth things over.

"Don't worry, your hair will tame down, Holly. If it's like most newly permed hair, it should be quite manageable in about a week . . . with these." And nonchalantly, she dumped a handful of conditioner samples into my purse.

A week?

She acted as though there was absolutely nothing wrong with that amount of time. I started to say I wanted my money back . . . no, what I really wanted was my old, straight hair back. But she was too busy greeting her next customer to notice my panic.

Frustrated, I paid and left. The instant I arrived home, I called Andie. "You have to come over!"

"Why? What's wrong?"

"Just hurry," I pleaded, filling her in on the horrid details.

She came over. Faster than ever before. With her makeup bag and scissors in tow.

When she started pulling the scissors out and snipping the air around my hair, I backed away. "Wait!"

"A little trim should help things." She seemed to be dying for the opportunity to whack away.

I peered into my dresser mirror. My hair had turned wild, all right.

Carrie, my flesh-and-blood sister, almost ten, poked her nose into my room. Stephanie, age eight, my youngest cousin-turned-stepsister, was right behind her. "Hey, who fried your hair?" Stephie asked.

Carrie and Stephie stood there staring at me,

their eyes growing wider with each second. "Eewie, reminds me of some wild animal!" Carrie shouted.

I reached out to grab her, but Uncle Jack, my stepdad, appeared in the hallway. (The uncle part came from the fact that he'd been married to my dad's sister before she died. So he wasn't a blood relative.)

Carrie yelled, "Don't touch me!"

I slammed the door. Muffled, anxious tones floated through the cracks, but I held my breath, hoping nobody would investigate. No one did.

Turning around, I pleaded with Andie for moral support.

"You've got to do something before tomorrow," she advised. "And fast." She'd situated herself on my window seat, stroking Goofey, my old tabby cat.

"So . . ." I began. "Besides cutting it all off, what do you suggest?"

"A light trim will do." Andie got up and pranced over to where I stood fussing with my mane. She held up her scissors. "Show me how much to trim."

I frowned and held my fingers about an inch apart. "This much?"

Andie shook her head. "Nope, that won't even cut it."

We both burst into giggles. Mostly nervous ones.

"Honest—I didn't mean to make a pun." She waved the scissors at me.

I pulled a piece of hair forward, let it brush against my face, then let it fall. The texture was unbelievably coarse. Even with the sample moisturizers from the beauty salon, I couldn't imagine ever getting my hair back to its normal, healthy sheen. "It's perfectly hopeless," I whispered.

"Not if we get the dead, dry ends off."

I sighed. "How many inches?"

She fooled with the back of my hair. After a few seconds she said, "At least six."

"Six inches?" I whirled around. "No way!"

"Don't freak," Andie said. "Now turn around, and I'll tap on your back where your hair would come."

I could feel her hand bumping my spine below my shoulder blades. "I don't know," I muttered. "Feels awfully short."

She picked up a strand of hair and held it high. "Look at this mess. Cutting it is the only possible remedy. And it's not the end of the world," she reminded me. "Hair always grows back."

She had a point. Only I didn't want to think about waiting for my hair to grow. "Cut no more than three inches," I commanded, watching nervously as she wielded her scissors.

Without another word, Andie began to snip away.

4

"So . . . what do you think?" Andie asked when she was finished.

I reached for a hand mirror and turned around, checking the back of my hair. "It's still too bushy."

"But you have to admit, it's better."

I combed through. "It's uneven, though—look!"

She inspected it. "You're right. Here, hold still, I'll straighten things out."

I was nervous. In fact, I shook with fright. Maybe having Andie cut my hair wasn't such a good idea. Maybe I should call a halt to things right now. Have it cut professionally . . .

"Uh, wait, Andie," I ventured.

She stopped cutting and looked at me in the mirror. "Why, what's wrong?"

"I don't think you should cut off any more," I said.

"Do you really think I'm going to let my

campaign manager run around looking like Einstein?" she said, laughing it off. "You've got to look cool if you're going to help me solicit votes."

"Right." I'd almost forgotten about managing her campaign. It seemed so trivial at the moment. "Look, maybe it would be better to have someone professional even it up."

"It'll be okay," she insisted. "I'll be careful not to cut off too much. I promise." I held my breath again, cringing with the sound of each snip of the scissors.

At last she was finished. A wave of relief rushed over me as she placed the scissors on the dresser.

"Now it's lots better," she said with delight.

I looked in the hand mirror, inspecting the trim job. My heart sank as I stared in horror. My hair, my beautiful hair, looked like a brier thicket. And the length? It came to about mid-back. My greatest fear had come true!

♥   ♥   ♥

In order to nurse my wounds, I asked Mom if I could eat supper in my room. No sense exposing myself to snide remarks from my brousins. Stan, age sixteen, Phil, just turned eleven, and Mark, now nine, were sure to find my frizzle-frazzle hair a target for jokes.

"Aw, honey, just pull it back in a braid or

something," Mom suggested.

"And what do I do with the rest of it?" I said, referring to the puffiness on top of my head. "It's like a bush!"

Mom tried to be helpful. "I'll run to the store after supper. Maybe I can find a hair reconstructer . . . something to treat the problem."

I sighed. Now my own mother was calling my hair a problem! "But is it okay if I eat in my room?" I pleaded.

She set the salad bowl down, her eyes squinting. Uh-oh, she was upset. "You should know better than to ask that, Holly-Heart. We're one big, happy family around here."

Happy for her, maybe. She hadn't been the brunt of constant teasing. And pranks. From the minute my uncle Jack married Mom last Thanksgiving, my cousins—his four kids—had seized every opportunity to make my life miserable. Starting with little miss snoopy Stephie and my diary. And Mark and Phil were constantly trying to get out of kitchen duty, not to mention hiding the TV remote so they could concentrate on their computer games. Nonstop. Last, but not least, was sneery Stan, who at his age should've known better than to humiliate me at every turn.

This was happy?

"Oh, Mom," I groaned. "Please let me?"

But she pointed to the dining room. "You heard me. Supper's on the table."

I ran upstairs to tie my hair back, steeling myself against insults sure to come.

And come they did. Beginning with the way Phil prayed over the food. "Dear Lord, bless this food to make us healthy and strong. And while you're at it, could you bless something else, too?" He paused dramatically. I could feel it coming . . . right down to my fried follicles!

Phil, of course, did not disappoint me. He barreled right on through. "Please, dear Lord, do something quick to help Holly's, uh . . . hair."

"Mom!" I blurted.

"Philip Patterson!" my stepdad said.

The prayer was over, that fact was obvious. Uncle Jack reprimanded Phil sternly, even made him apologize to me. Still, I resented being present at the table with everyone staring—or trying not to stare.

After supper, Mom was kind enough to let me off the hook for kitchen cleanup. I snickered when she chose Phil to take my place scraping dishes. Justice!

I reached for an extra sugar cookie and headed for my room, even though I longed to sit out on the front-porch swing. But it wasn't worth the risk. You never knew who might stroll by on an evening like this.

Back in front of my dresser mirror, I gawked at my mop. I couldn't remember spending this much time in front of a mirror . . . not ever.

I reached back and took out my hair band, then started brushing. Would the natural oils in my scalp kick in after a hundred strokes? Two hundred?

I brushed vigorously, then stopped to check. No oil, no nothing. After three hundred brush strokes and a very sore arm, I knew this frantic approach wasn't doing the trick. In fact, the brushing made my hair stick out even worse.

Then I remembered the sample conditioner packets and found my purse. "These better work," I mumbled to myself.

My image was on the line. Tomorrow was my first day as a high-school freshman.

With faint hope, I trudged to the bathroom.

5

Tuesday, September 3 – 2:00 A.M.: Here I am, sitting on my window seat in the middle of the night, waiting for the tenth dose of moisturizer to actually work on my hair. It's so quiet in the house—and strange being the only one awake. Shoot, I have to be up and ready for school in five hours. What a nightmare!

Andie, Paula, and Kayla will probably be wide awake and alert tomorrow, looking perfectly stunning in their new school clothes, having spent just a few minutes on their hair. . . .

I'm reading the back of the sample packet, and it honestly guarantees that rich botanical reconstructer ingredients will repair hair to its smoothest, shiniest, and most manageable state of health.

Yeah, well, I can only hope.

I'm going to leave this smelly goop on for another five minutes, and if it doesn't work, I'm shaving my head!

I can see it now—Andie freaking out. "How could you DO such a stupid thing?" she'll say.

"But . . . isn't slick bald in?" I'll answer, acting naïve, which I sort of am anyway.

Her eyes will do their roller-coaster number. "You can't be serious, Holly." She'll probably avoid me for the rest of the year. (And all I wanted to do was get a HEAD start!)

Enough—my humor is sick and so is my hair. It's time to go back to the bathroom and rinse this stuff out. I can't wait to see if this is the end of the fuzz. Here's hoping!

6

Mrs. Hibbard was outside sweeping her front walk when I passed her house the next morning. "Holly, your hair looks lovely," she called. "You must've gotten a good perm."

"Thank you," I replied, ignoring her comment about the perm being good. A power-perm oozing with oomph, able to leap long follicles, was a better way to describe it!

But, miraculously, my hair had turned out semi-okay. Thanks to a night spent applying a zillion moisture treatments. This morning I'd used Mom's hot styling brush. My hair was still a little too fluffy, but the shine and flexibility had returned. I was a walking, breathing hair reconstructer ad.

Mrs. Hibbard hadn't said anything about the bags under my eyes, but I knew they were obvious. What a way to start my freshman year. I'd grabbed two cans of caffeine-packed pop on my way out the door and stashed them in my schoolbag. The caffeine would keep me going at least till lunch.

As I boarded the bus, I searched for Andie, Paula, and Kayla. Mostly older kids—upperclassmen—sat in the back of the bus. I found a seat close to the front, wondering if my friends had gotten a ride to school.

Stan had.

Somehow, my stepbrother had talked Mom into letting him have her car for the first day of school. But had he included me? Guess that's what happens when tenth graders get pushed up to the second rung of the high-school ladder. One rung higher made a big difference—in attitude.

What if . . .

I daydreamed about how things might've been. This moment, I might be riding off to my last, fabulous year of junior high. Top of the totem pole. Right where Andie and all the rest of us cool freshmen belonged.

♥ ♥ ♥

The bus came to a stop across from Dressel Hills High School. As I waited to get off, I noticed the Miller twins standing on the school steps with Danny, Billy, and Andie.

Andie spotted me as I came off the bus. "Holly!" she called, and I ran across the street to meet her. "Wow, your hair looks great!"

"What you really mean is it looks poofy."

"C'mon, Holly, it's not that bad."

"Thanks," I said, "but you won't believe what I went through to get it semi-manageable."

She cocked her head and studied me. "You look wiped out, girl."

"You'd be tired, too, with just five hours of Zs."

Andie grinned. "You're here; that's all that matters."

I sighed, glancing at the twins heading up the school steps. "Getting stuck riding alone on the bus the first day of school when your best friend is—"

"Don't give me grief over that," Andie interrupted. "It wasn't my idea."

I felt foolish for saying anything. "Just forget it," I muttered. And we turned toward the steps of the enormous old high school. I, for one, was definitely not looking forward to this day.

Once inside, we headed for our lockers, assigned during recent registration. Andie's was close to Paula and Kayla Miller's—a random assignment from the school office. The threesome chattered about the day and their schedules while Danny and Billy hovered nearby. My locker was practically a mile away—down the hall. I trudged off by myself, feeling lonely. And puffy-haired.

A pit stop in the bathroom confirmed my worries. My hair was not only puffy, it had started to frizz up—and out! Now that it was shorter, there wasn't the length to weigh it down.

I decided to brush it out, hairspray and all, and

pull it back against my head in a tight, single braid. Running the hot water, I held my brush under the faucet. Frantically, I plastered my hair against my temples, as wet and straight as possible.

Perfect. Now if I could just do this after every class. Sure, it was a hassle, but it beat looking like something out of a circus freak show.

♥   ♥   ♥

Homeroom, Room 202, with Mr. Irving seemed strange. A male homeroom teacher? It just didn't fit. Not for me, anyway. Oh, there'd been men teachers in junior high—Mr. Ross, the infamous science teacher with only one necktie, and the adorable student teacher last spring, Mr. Barnett. But homeroom? Never!

Maybe that's why things were so unsettling. But maybe it was something else. Andie was down the hall in Room 210—Miss Shaw's homeroom. My best friend and I had never been separated in school. Not like this.

I took a deep breath, trying to push out negative thoughts. Once seated, I got my backpack situated and located a pen and my three-ring binder just as Jared and Amy-Liz entered the classroom holding hands. The sight of them together struck me hard. I mean, ever since I'd first met Jared halfway through seventh grade, he'd flirted with me. Lots. Even long after we'd decided to be just friends, he never seemed willing to let me go. Until now . . .

Jared and Amy-Liz sat across from each other, and I saw that he had eyes for only one person now: Amy-Liz Thompson. Cute, with naturally wavy, blond hair, my petite friend also had a high, clear soprano voice, not to mention a sparkling personality.

The thought of my first boyfriend interested in someone else made me feel even worse. I guess when it came right down to understanding why I felt this way, I was basically in the dark. But I knew one thing so far: life as a freshman stunk!

"Good morning," Mr. Irving said. "I have a number of things to pass out to you today. Please bear with me as I do the required paper-pushing thing."

Bear with me? Paper-pushing thing? Where'd they find this guy? But the more I studied him, the more I realized he reminded me of someone's uncle. He was almost parental, I guess you could say.

There were zillions of things to be announced, and my attention wandered a bit while Mr. Irving listed various deadlines, mostly for the return of the papers he'd just distributed. But something about him—maybe his ongoing humorous remarks—reminded me of Uncle Jack.

My ears perked up when he mentioned the election of freshman officers for student council. Jared and Amy-Liz seemed to pay attention for the first time, too.

"One week from now—and you'll be hearing more about this," Mr. Irving explained, "we'll be running election campaigns for this year's freshman class. For student council."

Jared raised his hand. "Can anyone run?"

"Absolutely," Mr. Irving said. "America is still a free country." Laughter splashed through the classroom.

I glanced at Jared, who was whispering something to Amy-Liz. Was he going to run? And if so, would Amy-Liz handle his campaign?

I'd already promised to help Andie and had assured her I wouldn't run. Maybe I should've thought it through. Maybe it wasn't too late to change my mind and run against Andie and Jared. And beat them both!

On top of everything—bad hair day included—I expected tons of homework. No disappointment here. High-school teachers knew how to pile it on. They weren't easing us lowly freshmen into high-school life very gradually.

I was feeling totally stressed out by lunchtime with only five minutes between classes to wet down my hair and go to my locker. I'd saved three places in the cafeteria, hoping Andie, Paula, and Kayla might show up and share the woes of their first morning back at school.

Suddenly I noticed a pixie-haired girl standing motionless in the doorway of the cafeteria. Her eyes were a blank stare. And a beautiful dog—a golden retriever—stood at her side.

I watched as the dog deftly guided her through

the maze of tables and students to the teacher-monitor. Observing the girl, I felt ashamed. My feelings of contempt for these halls of higher learning and the cruel way life had seemingly treated me—forcing me out of my cozy junior-high nest, not to mention the over-perming of my hair—well, all that seemed unimportant as I watched the blind student.

I began to eat my lunch, contemplating life without the fabulous sense of sight—thinking how it would be having to depend on another person or a guide dog for my mobility—whew! The thought of such a thing made the imposed move to high school seem trivial.

Ditto for hair problems.

7

Curious about the blind girl, I started to get up to go introduce myself. That's when Andie and Paula showed up.

"Hey, Holly," they said together, each of them pulling out a chair across the table from me.

Andie seemed a bit startled when she looked at me. "What happened to your hair?" she asked. "It looked really good this morning."

"It started frizzing out, so I decided this was the best I could do."

"Oh, but it's very stylish," Paula offered. "Quite tomboyish, actually."

"Wish I had some mousse to weigh it down." Quickly, I told Paula the perm story, playing it down in light of the blind girl who sat a few tables away.

"Thank goodness for modern hair repair," Andie said, laughing. "Holly was up all night applying moisturizers."

There was a glint of recognition in Paula's eyes. "I've certainly had my share of such discouraging things."

I smiled at her comment. Paula and her twin, Kayla, had a very unique way of expressing themselves.

Suddenly I noticed there were no lunch trays or brown bags for either of them. "Not eating lunch today?"

They glanced at each other, smiling. "Oh, we just had burgers with some guys," Andie said.

"What guys?" I looked around.

Andie explained. "Actually, it wasn't just guys. Amy-Liz and Kayla were along, too."

"Oh, yes, it was really very surprising how it all came about," Paula spoke up.

"How *what* came about?" I asked.

Paula continued. "A group of us got charged up about student council elections—"

"In two weeks," Andie interrupted.

"Yes," Paula said, "and we decided to have sort of a prayer conference about it. So all of us zipped over to the Soda Straw, you know, and prayed about how we could influence our school for God."

"Over burgers?" I asked.

Andie's dark eyes twinkled. She stopped for a moment and spoke to Paula, but I couldn't hear what she was saying because I was chewing potato chips.

Paula burst out an explanation. "Since we couldn't have prayer on school grounds, we took our meeting to a public eating place."

"Who's we?" I asked, wondering why I'd been excluded.

"Jared, Amy-Liz, Kayla, and us . . . you know, the kids most interested in running for student council," Paula said.

"Oh." I'd told Andie a few days ago I wasn't interested. Not this year—too much homework. And I had to keep up my grades. Obviously she thought I didn't care about any aspect of it.

"So," Andie piped up, "we decided that as many Christians should run as possible. What do you think, Holly?"

I nodded, feeling completely left out at this point. "Well, I think it's a great idea. Hey, why don't we turn the elections into a crusade?" My words gave me away. I sounded way too sarcastic.

"Holly? What's wrong?" Paula asked.

I shrugged. "High school's just a little over-whelming, I guess. Haven't *you* gotten tons of homework already today?"

Paula shook her head. "It may seem rather unfair, but being a sophomore helps. Honestly, I can't say that I've experienced the same sort of homework load that I hear most ninth graders talking about."

"Don't call us ninth graders," Andie retorted. "We're freshmen."

Paula smiled, and when her lips parted, I noticed her perfectly straight, white teeth. I don't know why I always noticed that part of Paula and her twin, but somehow their pearly whites always got my attention.

"Did you and Kayla wear braces when you were younger?" I asked.

"We never wore them," Paula cooed.

"Let's face it," Andie said. "They have teeth to die for. And poor me—I just found out I have to get braces. Can you believe it? At my age? I've got to wear them for nearly *three years*—ugh!"

I laughed. "Well, your smile should be beautiful in time for senior year."

She sighed. "At least I'll have *one* year of high school without braces."

"Well," Paula said, glancing at her watch, "I have a class now. See you two later."

"Bye." I expected Andie to stay a few minutes and chat, but to my surprise, she followed Paula right out of the cafeteria with only a fleeting wave back to me.

I finished off my Jell-O salad and cookie, wondering how things between Andie and me could've gone from a super tight friendship . . . to this. What had happened?

On my way to the kitchen to return my tray and dump my trash, I noticed the blind girl again. She was sitting at a table with several other kids. None of them were talking to her. I wanted to go over and start a conversation, but I bumped into Billy Hill near the kitchen.

"I'm thinking of running for class treasurer." He rubbed his hands together. "You know how money and I mix."

"When did you decide this?"

"Today at the Soda Straw." He shifted his

weight from one foot to the other, like he was too shy to continue.

"Billy, what is it?"

"Well, I heard you were helping Andie with her campaign and stuff, but I thought I'd ask." Billy's tall, muscular frame hovered over me, his blond bangs flopping across his forehead.

"Ask what?"

"For some expert advice about slogans. Paula says you're good at making up things like that."

Paula said that? I was shocked.

"I'll see what I can do," I said.

"Thanks," he called as I hurried off.

My next class was French, but I wanted to make a quick trip to the girls' rest room. I could feel my hair drying out.

Searching for my schedule, I discovered that Room 202—my homeroom—was the location for French I. And Mr. Irving was the teacher.

♥   ♥   ♥

In the space of two minutes, I learned the correct way to pronounce *oui, n'est-ce pas, mademoiselle,* and *au revoir.* By the end of the hour I was asking questions in French, like What time is it? What is your name? How are you? and Do you speak French?—with the right amount of throaty sound to my Rs. It was more fun than I ever dreamed. In fact, there was only one problem with my first encounter with French: Andie hadn't shared it with me.

Weeks ago we'd had a major discussion about foreign languages. Andie tried to convince me that she shouldn't take French since she was fluent in Spanish. "Why bother?" she'd said.

"If you want to go to college and study music," I argued, "you need four years of some language."

"Then it should be German—the language of the great composers," she'd decided. But when it came time to register, she had ignored the language classes.

The truth was, at least the way I saw it, Andie hadn't really decided to take the college prep track. For as long as I could remember, Andie had talked of getting married and being a mother someday. That was her number one goal for life. That and teaching a few piano students.

Andie's goal was perfect for her. Sometimes hearing her talk about raising a large family and cooking great Mexican meals for them made me wonder if I was doing the right thing by reaching for a career in free-lance writing. Andie's uncomplicated, cozy future-to-be appealed to me. *Some* days.

After school, Andie, Paula, and Kayla stopped at my locker. "We need to start planning my campaign," Andie said. "You know, get a jump on things."

"Okay, so plan," I answered, laughing.

Andie grinned. "You've always been more popular than me, Holly. But I have every confidence that your fab-u-lous handling of my election campaign is going to make me president of the freshman class."

Kayla interrupted us, reaching over to touch my hair. "This is definitely permed," she said.

"No kidding," Andie said, launching off on her explanation of how I'd spent all night taming it.

"Oh, dear." Kayla put her hand over her heart. "You must be fairly exhausted."

Andie stepped closer. "Are you tired, Holly-Heart?" she asked, using the nickname my mother gave me long ago.

"Well"—I yawned—"I guess I'm too tired to plan strategy for your election campaign tonight, if that's what you mean."

"It can wait." Andie shifted her books.

I closed my locker door. "Tomorrow?"

"Sure," Andie said rather grudgingly. And the threesome headed up the hall to their lockers.

Paula and Kayla started chattering about making banners and signs as they walked away. I tried not to let it bother me. But that was supposed to be the campaign manager's job. My job.

8

Thursday after school Andie and I met at her house to make banners and, in general, plan her campaign. "I think we need lots more help," she said. "Don't you?"

I agreed. "I can round up plenty of kids." I glanced around at the kitchen table. "But what about supplies? I don't think there's enough poster board here to make—"

"Can't we get started with what we do have?" she interrupted.

I shrugged. Something was obviously bugging her. "Sure, whatever."

We made large, vertical posters and wide, horizontal pennants that tapered to a point. Some with sayings she'd thought up, others with more humorous slogans from my zany brain. One was "Vote for Andie, She'll Come in Handy."

"That's too weird, Holly," she said. "Besides, you're showing off. This isn't a creative-writing class, you know."

I shook my head. The girl was behaving like a spoiled brat. Refusing to fight, I bit my tongue. "Have it your way," I replied and reached for the glue.

And that's precisely how things were between us for the whole first hour. A negative and not-so-subtle undercurrent was evident.

After five posters were completed, we tried to discuss her campaign speech. Andie had made up her mind about that, too. "You're going to write it," she insisted.

"But it's your speech."

"You're the writer," she whined.

Now I was really upset. "Look, Andie, can't you do something to solicit votes? After all, it was *your* idea to run for office."

Andie gave a disgusted grunt. "Fine, don't help me. I'll get Paula to write my speech."

"Hey, that'll work . . . if you want to sound like something out of *Jane Eyre*," I spouted. "Go ahead."

"What?" Amazingly, she didn't get it, so I pointed out the way the Miller twins talked.

"Yeah, I see what you mean," she agreed, twirling a dark curl. "So won't you please, please write my speech?"

Andie was desperate. So I budged—an inch. "Okay, I'll edit it," I said. "But I won't write it."

She grinned, obviously pleased. However, her change in attitude didn't last long. Paula and Kayla Miller showed up a few minutes later and, honestly, Andie began to side with them. Over everything.

I was furious. For one thing, she liked their suggestions better than mine. For another thing, I felt a cliquish thing going on between them—creating a swell in the current. The undertow was growing to tidal wave proportions—and I was getting sucked out to sea.

♥   ♥   ♥

To make matters worse for Andie, on Friday the very cool Jeff Kinney tossed his hat into the race. Posters kept showing up everywhere—"Don't Be a Ninny, Vote for Jeff Kinney."

On top of that, Jeff was making campaign promises. Big ones. Stuff like a pizza bash at his election party. And free pop on Fridays. Every Friday for the whole year!

Such a smooth talker. Jeff had it all over Andie in that department. Not that Andie wasn't articulate, but Jeff had a real way with words—something akin to a used-car salesman.

I wondered how Andie could compete. Of course, I knew the answer. There was no way.

Funny thing. People kept coming up to me, saying I should run. "Why don't you?" Jared asked, without flirting (probably because my hair looked so pathetic).

When I explained my reasons—the homework,

especially algebra, and the grades thing—he seemed to understand. Sort of. Then, right as he was about to leave, he said something obnoxious. "That's you under all that . . . uh, fuzz, isn't it, Holly?"

"Get lost," I muttered.

"C'mon, I was only joking."

"Yeah, right," I blubbered. "Go joke with Amy-Liz." And I turned on my heel.

Later that afternoon, Marcia Greene, one of the student editors for the high-school paper, *The Summit*, told me she was glad I wasn't running for student council. "Because," she said, "you're a good writer, and I'm going to need lots of fresh-man-related articles this semester. Maybe some teacher profiles, too."

As an eighth grader I'd played journalist and loved it. Even interviewed a handsome student teacher once . . .

That seemed like decades ago. But writing for a high-school paper? Now, that would be really fabulous. If only I could get my mind off Andie and the weird way she and the Miller twins were acting.

I was beginning to think that the close friendship Andie, Paula, and I had experienced during the past few months was only a dream. And it hurt.

9

I loved Saturdays.

These days, Mom usually let us sleep in. Things had been much different before Mom married Uncle Jack, though. Carrie and I would get up and clean our rooms, help with other chores, then go with Mom to get groceries in the afternoon.

Now on Saturdays we cleaned our rooms but after a hearty family breakfast. Brunch. Then kitchen cleanup. And that was the extent of the chores. The rest of the day we were free to hang out, talk on the phone, go to the mall . . . do whatever.

Mom no longer worked at the law firm as a paralegal—Uncle Jack supported us now. Mom loved being a full-time wife and mother. Often, she made trips to the grocery store three or four times a week (cooking for eight took three times the food). But Saturday was never a grocery day anymore. And all the other chores got divvied up among six kids, to be done during the week. So things zipped along quite smoothly at 207 Downhill Court.

Weekends were an event at the Meredith-Patterson household. Try getting six kids and two adults to agree on an activity or a game. *Any* activity or game. Getting all of us to show up for brunch at the same time was a miracle.

Fortunately, Stephie, Mark, Phil, and Stan had always been close cousins to Carrie and me. Even though they'd lived with their parents in Pennsylvania before Aunt Marla died—and we were out here in Colorado—we always loved getting together. Summer and Christmas. Every year.

The hardest part about having four cousins turn into stepsiblings was the way it increased the decibel level in the house. Frequently on Saturdays I'd awaken to Carrie and Stephie giggling loudly in their room down the hall. Or Stephie's CD player going full blast—the reason why I was awake this very minute!

Besides that, my brain hurt as I thought about Andie. Her stubbornness was getting out of hand. Rolling over, I grabbed the blanket and pressed it over my ear. Stephie's silly CD kept going. I tried to block out the sound and resume my sleepy state by thinking of pastures of wildflowers, lovely mountain streams—anything to relax. No use. Stephie's ditty-tune went straight to my brain.

Frustrated, I leaped out of bed and made a mad dash to the bedroom down the hall. "Okay, you two," I said, leaning against the door, "cut the noise."

I pushed the door open, but the room was empty. I hurried to the bookshelf near Stephie's bed and turned off the obnoxious song.

Silence.

Perfect. I sat down on Carrie's unmade bed, wishing it were this easy to stop the noise in my head about Andie. She'd become so demanding, only wanted things her way.

My ideas weren't good enough anymore. So . . . basically, I didn't care. Paula could run the show for her. Or Kayla. Or even Amy-Liz. Except, no, Amy-Liz was campaigning for Jared, of course. He was running for vice-president. Couldn't quite figure that out, because Jared would easily win over Andie. He was far more popular. And when it came to student council, popularity got the votes.

As for Andie, she didn't stand a chance. Not against Jeff Kinney.

Suddenly Carrie screamed. "Mommy! Holly's in our room."

"Yeah," Stephie hollered. "Make her get out. It's supposed to be private."

I leaped off Carrie's bed and hurried out of the room.

The little twerps followed me down the hall and into my bedroom before I could close the door.

Carrie put her hands on her hips and glared at me. She was a mini-image of me. Except now, her hair was the longest in the house. "Okay, confess—what were you doing?"

Stephie frowned, her chestnut hair brushing against her cheek. "Were you snooping?"

I sat on my lavender-and-white-lace canopy bed and smiled. "Look, girls, it's as simple as this. I was daydreaming."

Stephie's freckles twitched. "You mean you weren't trying to find our top secret—"

"Shh!" Carrie blurted.

Stephie looked worried. "What? I didn't spoil anything, did I?"

"Just be quiet," Carrie commanded.

Stephie nodded. "On my princess honor," she said, raising her right hand.

"Don't say that!" Carrie howled, grabbing Stephie by the arm and pulling her out of my room.

I grinned, peeking down the hall. Before I closed my door I heard Carrie reprimand Stephie further. Only now in a whisper. "You don't want anyone to know about our secret pact, do you?"

Settling down on my cozy window seat, I thought about Carrie's words and smiled.

It hadn't been so long ago that Andie and I had our own secret pact. A pact of friendship called the Loyalty Papers.

Funny, as you get older, those kinds of things—although heartfelt at the time—become virtually unnecessary. But in a childish sort of way, I was glad I'd saved our old pact. It was special beyond words. At least, that's how I'd always viewed it.

I went to look for the box of childhood treasures stowed under my bed. Sure enough, the Loyalty Papers were tucked away for posterity, and I pulled them out for a comforting escape into the past.

Andie? She'd been a true-blue best friend for the most part up until around seventh grade. That's when I'd freaked out and torn up our Loyalty Papers. But, angry as I was, the bond of friendship had shone through. There had been a copy of the pact hidden under my mattress.

These days, Loyalty Papers were no longer in effect. We'd grown past our need for strict rules for conducting a perfect best-friendship. Way past. Maybe so far past that a glimpse into the carefree days of our childhood—together—might help things between us.

I ran downstairs to the kitchen, grabbed the portable phone, and called Andie.

She answered on the first ring. "Hello?"

"Hey," I said. "I was just thinking."

"Yeah?"

"You remember those Loyalty Papers we wrote in third grade?"

She gasped. "Holly! You have to be reverting."

"I'm what?"

"You know, you're going backward," she said. "Is it the high-school thing? The trauma of being pushed out of junior high?"

"The what?"

She tried to explain. "Sometimes people revert to a safer, more secure moment in their past to . . . uh, buffer their present situation. Is that it, Holly? Think about it, please?"

"Look, all I wanted to do was have you come over sometime today, just for old times' sake."

She exhaled into the phone. "I'm so busy. In case you forgot, I'm running for the highest office of the Dressel Hills freshman class."

"Oh." She knocked the wind out of me.

Neither of us spoke for a moment. Then she said, "Are you coming to *my* house? Paula and Kayla are here helping with more posters and stuff."

"Why should I? You're not interested in my suggestions anyhow."

The silence made my heart pound. I wanted her to coax me, to plead with me to come.

"Fine. Have it your way," Andie said finally and hung up.

Devastation set in, but it was my own fault. The Miller twins and Andie were having a party-down weekend. Without me.

10

After brunch the mail came, and with it, a snail-mail letter from Sean. I ran to my room and opened the envelope.

Dear Holly,

Thanks for your letter. It's always great to hear from you.

I'm going to be honest with you. I don't think you have anything to worry about as far as high school is concerned. Maybe by now you've found that to be true.

Looking back on my freshman year, I remember feeling twinges of anticipation and worry. Mostly about the grading scale, I think. A score of 94 was a B+—that took some getting used to. What's the grading scale there?

About initiation, I suppose the worst thing that could happen is you forget next year what it was like being a freshman and dish out some of the same stuff yourself.

But I have faith in you, Holly. You have a good

heart. And always will.

I stopped reading and remembered the craziness I'd initiated during summer youth camp. Wow, I wondered what Sean would think of that. Turning the page of his letter, I read on.

> *Just be on the alert to what might (or could) happen. I'll bet your friend Andie will help watch out for pranks, too. How's she doing, by the way?*

I stopped reading again and thought about my trip to see Daddy in California this past summer. Andie and I had gone there together. What a crazy time that was, too, but we learned some important things about life . . . and about avoiding little white lies, no matter what.

Sean would be surprised to know that Andie was running for class president. Strangely enough, the fact still surprised me. I turned back to Sean's letter.

> *Let me know how your first week of high school goes. What's your favorite class so far? Do you have any interesting teachers this year?*
>
> *My calculus teacher is having chemotherapy. He's really a terrific guy. We've had a couple private talks about the Lord after school. Unfortunately, Mr. Fremont has cancer. His hair is starting to come out, and several students have decided to shave their heads. What do you think? Should I shave mine? Tell me the truth, okay?*
>
> *I really miss you, Holly. Please write back soon.*
> *Yours, Sean*

I refolded the letter and carefully slipped it back inside the envelope. What a great guy! Too bad Sean didn't live in Dressel Hills or at least somewhere in Colorado. Somewhere closer.

I glanced fondly at the cream-colored envelope and his handwriting. Clean, strong strokes, and easy to read, unlike some guys' I knew.

Dear, dear Sean, I thought. He wants me to decide if he should shave his head. A thoughtful gesture, a noble plan. And not a bad idea, especially since I wouldn't have to witness it. A cop-out, though. What if I did have to see it every day? Would that make a difference?

This talk of head shaving made me think about my own kinky mess. Would my hair grow back curly or straight if I shaved it off? A frightening thought—a bald girl. Yikes!

Quickly, I got up and looked in the dresser mirror. My hair looked worse than ever—sticking out everywhere—even with a couple of days' worth of scalp oil. Usually I washed my hair every other day. It wasn't as oily as some girls' hair. Amy-Liz for one. She had to wash her hair every time she turned around. If I had to wash mine every day, with hair as thick as this, I'd be spending half my life drying it.

With that thought, I grabbed my robe and headed for the shower. If I washed my mop several times today, maybe the shampoo would weaken the perm. It was worth a try!

♥　♥　♥

Later that afternoon Andie called. Could she come over? Sure, I told her, even though I was still peeved at her. The girl sounded frantic.

I waited out on the front porch, letting the air dry my damp hair. The sky was scattered with high, feathery clouds that Daddy had always said were for the angels. Featherbeds. I smiled, glad that Daddy was a Christian now. And to think that Sean's older brother had been partly responsible. Prayer really does change things . . . people, too.

Finally Andie arrived. I watched her get off the city bus and run across the street. I stood up and went to meet her. "What's wrong?" I asked.

"Everything. Jeff Kinney's making all those promises, you know." She marched up on the porch and sat down on the swing. "I heard his dad's a soda dealer; they'll stock the pop machines, no problem." Her words spilled out. "Oh, Holly, it's hopeless. There's no way I can compete!"

"So what's wrong with good, solid representation? You know, listening to students' pet peeves? You could make a complaint box and promise to read every letter. Then do whatever it takes to change things . . . solve the problems."

"That's hokey." Andie stopped the swing and stared at me. "You sound like I'm a Miss Fix-It. I'm not running a Dr. Laura show here, for your information."

I nodded. "But there's nothing wrong with offering—and promising—to do your best to represent the wishes of the freshman class."

She shrugged, then pushed her toe against the porch floor. "It's just that I can't compete with a rich kid. Jeff's got the kind of backing I could only dream of."

"I know," I said softly. "It doesn't seem fair."

She talked about how raunchy it was for Jeff Kinney to run his campaign like that. Bribery. And not knowing what else to say, I agreed.

We sat in silence for a few minutes. Then I said, "Why do you think Jared's not running against you?"

"I don't know, guess he's trying to be nice—for a change. He's running for vice-president, and so far no one's competing against him. And did you hear? Amy-Liz is running for secretary."

"Really?" This was news.

"Yep, she wants to make sure she sticks close to Jared. And personally, I think they make a good couple."

Better than you and Jared, she was probably thinking.

"Well, I hope he's treating her better than he treated me. It gets old knowing your boyfriend's flirting with every girl in the school."

Andie faced me. "That's the amazing thing, you know. Jared's actually quit flirting. It's like some miracle."

I laughed. "I wouldn't go that far, but he does seem more mature. But then, I thought that about him last year. Maybe we should wait and see if the newness wears off."

"Speaking of new, how's Sean Hamilton?" She

studied me with her dark, inquisitive eyes.

"I got another letter today," I said. "He's answered all my letters so far—email messages, too. And he asked about you."

Her face broke into a wide grin. "He did?"

"Uh-huh. Hold on. I'll read it to you." I hurried inside.

When I came back, Stan was sitting on the front-porch step. He'd brought out some soda for Andie and was guzzling a can of his own. But he wasn't making eye contact with her, so I knew he was being a jerk. As always.

I folded the letter from Sean and stuffed it inside my jeans. Andie patted the spot beside her on the swing, and a few minutes later Stan left.

"What's with him?" I asked.

"Try madly in love." She laughed. "With himself."

I snickered. Andie's comment was a fitting diagnosis of Stan's problem. When I was sure he was gone, I pulled the letter out of my pocket and began reading.

At the end of the letter, when I read that Sean missed me, Andie carried on. "Aw, how sweet," she said. "It must feel really great having a guy who cares enough to write you letters like that."

I held the letter against my heart. "Sean's the best."

She was grinning. "So when will you see him next?"

"Wish I knew. But for now, since I'm too young

to date, this might be the best thing. A long-distance friendship."

"C'mon, you can read between the lines, Holly. This guy likes you—really likes you!"

"So who said anything's wrong with starting out as good friends? I think I prefer it to the mushy stuff."

For a moment Andie didn't respond; then she looked at me sadly. "I guess I thought Stan and I had a chance for a solid friendship like that."

"Maybe you will someday," I offered. "But you two went separate ways, right?"

She nodded. "And honestly, things feel good this way—boyfriendless."

"Having a guy in our lives—at our age—is overrated. Besides, two weeks from now you could be freshman class president and too busy." I meant it to cheer her up.

"If I could just think of something to promise—a really great campaign pledge. Maybe then I'd have a fighting chance." She leaned back in the swing and stared at the sky.

With all my heart, I wished I could give her that. A fighting chance. My childhood best friend deserved it.

I couldn't help but grin as we sat there. It felt like old times between us as the afternoon sun shone down on Dressel Hills.

I was getting caught up in the feeling of having her back—that Andie and I hadn't lost anything, not really—when the most amazing idea hit me. The perfect campaign promise for Andie's speech.

"I've got it!" I jumped out of the porch swing. "I guarantee this'll get you elected."

Andie couldn't sit still. "What?" She got up and started dancing around the porch with me before I could even speak the words.

11

When Andie calmed down I told her my plan. "Here's what you have to promise the freshman class," I said.

"Out with it," she hollered.

"You have to promise to do away with initiation this year. You know, get us freshmen off the hook."

Her eyes grew wide. "That's incredible! But how do I pull it off? I mean, won't I have to talk to a bunch of seniors about this? Especially the most popular ones?"

"Probably. They're the ones who set up the pranks and stuff that goes on," I said. "Then it filters down through the juniors and sophomores . . . like that."

She twirled around in the middle of my porch. "This is so cool. You're a genius."

"Thank you, thank you." I bowed repeatedly, hamming it up.

Suddenly Andie scooted up onto the porch railing, balancing herself there. "There's only one problem. How will I do it? How can I possibly bribe the seniors?"

"Somehow you have to get them to waive initiation this year," I replied. "It's not fair in the first place because we're supposed to be in junior high. You could start out by reminding them of that."

Andie's eyes dropped. "I just don't know how we could talk them out of it. Maybe it isn't such a good idea, after all."

"We could suggest that they initiate the sophomores—they'd be getting it now if we hadn't been moved up," I said, thinking of Stan.

"Hey, you're right. Maybe I'll talk to Marcia Greene. Doesn't she have a brother who's a senior?"

"What about Shauna and Joy?" I said. "Don't they have older sisters—seniors, too?"

"And there's a bunch of seniors in the church youth group"—Andie was getting excited again—"maybe they'd help us."

We dashed inside for some ice cream. Time for celebration.

Mom was sorting through the kitchen pantry when we slid up to the bar stools. She turned and smiled. "You two certainly look happy."

Andie and I grinned at each other. "I think we've stumbled onto something to help get Andie elected," I said.

Mom simply had to hear what we were up to. "Sounds like a big undertaking to me," she said after we filled her in. "I'd hate to be the one to approach those haughty seniors at Dressel Hills High. Especially that Zye Greene."

"Zye?" Andie and I said in unison. "You mean Marcia Greene's brother?"

Mom nodded, her eyes squinting a little. "Zye Greene the second. He pretty much runs the show over there."

I wasn't sure how Mom knew so much. "How do you know this guy . . . Zye?"

Andie burst into laughter.

Mom chuckled a little. "Well, Zye, Sr., is a highly respected member of the Dressel Hills school board. In fact, he's the one who got the ball rolling for the ninth graders to move up to high school."

"Freshmen," Andie and I said together.

"Yes, you are definitely freshmen," Mom acknowledged. "It's just a little difficult for a mother to adjust to these sophisticated labels." She went back to organizing the pantry.

"Wow." I headed for the freezer. "What do you think? Could we get Marcia's brother to help us call off initiation?"

"We'll give it our best shot." Andie reached for the phone book.

"Who're you going to call?" I asked, dishing up some strawberry ice cream for two.

"Zye, the guy—our main man."

"Good thinking."

Andie scooped up a spoonful of ice cream while she looked in the phone book under the Gs.

"There aren't any Zye Greenes listed," she said, looking up.

"The number might be unlisted," Mom explained. "Maybe you should talk to Marcia on Monday."

"Aw, Mom!" I wailed. "We have to get things rolling now, or we'll never get Andie's campaign speech ready."

Andie was smiling like a chimp, showing all her teeth. "Hey, this is good news, Holly-Heart. You're worried about my speech. Does this mean you'll help me write it after all?"

"I'm speechless, er . . . you know." Oops, wrong choice of words.

Andie stared at me. "C'mon, Holly, I need you. Please?" Our eyes met. And all at once we were very close. Like little kids. I felt that I had a best friend forever. Andie needed my writing to make her speech fly. And I was the writer, like she said.

"Okay, Andie, you win," I said at last. "I'll write your speech."

"Yes!" She raised her hands high over her head.

I grabbed a tablet off the desk in the corner of the kitchen. "Now all I need is a sharpened pencil."

Andie hopped off the stool and found a pencil in a can on the desk. "This is so cool," she announced, hugging me.

Not for one second did I wish I were running

against her. Not anymore. I actually wanted to do this—write my best friend's speech, being Andie's campaign manager. With all my heart I wanted to.

Nothing else mattered.

Monday morning. Bad news.

Andie stopped at my locker first thing. She looked depressed. "We've got a problem," she said. "I talked to Zye Greene this morning. Man, what a jerk. How can his sister be so sweet? Anyway, this guy . . . he's got a major case of senioritis."

I groaned.

Andie continued. "He made it *so* obvious that he did not want some puny peon freshman asking him dumb questions. Zye said no senior alive—at least not in Dressel Hills—would agree to dump initiation. In fact, he let me in on a little secret."

I closed my locker door. "What's that?"

"He said this year's initiation was going to be tougher than ever." Andie's eyes bugged out. "Because, as he put it, 'freshmen have never darkened the doors of this high school.' Are we in for it or what?"

I didn't know what to say. It looked like my

plan had fallen flat. And to make things worse, I'd spent most of the weekend writing Andie's speech, focusing on the promise of no initiation. "So . . . now what do we do?"

Paula and Kayla were headed our way. "Have you discussed this with anyone else?" I asked Andie, nodding in the twins' direction.

"Being sophomores, Paula and Kayla loved your idea," Andie said. "They think none of us— not even tenth-grade students—should get initiated this year. It's degrading to the human spirit."

Sounded like something the Miller girls would say.

"Well, they'd be going through it if we weren't here," I whispered.

"It's either us or them," Andie said, meaning our sophomore friends.

Now the Miller twins were standing on either side of us. "Good morning," Paula said, sporting a new pair of denim overalls with a light-pink shirt. Kayla wore new Capri pants, tan with a white shirt.

"Hey," I said.

Andie smiled. "We've run into a slight snag."

The twins leaned in for the details, and while Andie explained things, I pushed my baseball cap down hard on my head. Wearing a hat worked quite well these days, with it smashing down the kinks in my hair.

Kayla must have noticed. "How goes the war?" she asked, eyeing my head.

I ignored the lame comment.

Paula, however, was a bit more sympathetic. "The tomboy look is very in, you know."

"Perfect," I cooed back.

But Andie had the jitters. She wanted to discuss our next move, so I paved the way for her to talk. "What about the seniors at our church . . . remember? Shouldn't we talk to them about initiation?"

"Haven't decided yet," Andie said. "Maybe if enough of us got together it would help. How many churchgoing freshmen do we know, anyway?"

We listed the Christian kids—Jared, Amy-Liz, Billy, Shauna, Joy, Andie, and me. Seven of us.

"Well, that's a good start," Andie said. "But we have to get going on this, because tomorrow's our class meeting."

"You're right," Kayla said, blinking her made-up eyes. "I've been hearing that Jeff Kinney's making some pretty impressive promises."

"Yeah, we heard," I said glumly.

"So what'll we do?" Andie asked.

"Let's try and have lunch with some seniors today," I suggested. "You know, just casually—get to know them."

"Cool," Andie said.

"We'll help spread the word," Paula said.

Spreading the word would be a relatively easy chore since the high school was reflective of our ski village. Small. There were only about three hundred students total—counting freshmen.

The bell rang. Andie, Paula, and Kayla sped off

to their individual homerooms. I hurried to Room 202, hoping my newly attained bond with Andie would not dissolve in a brush with senioritis.

In homeroom I sat through announcements. My ears perked up when Mr. Irving began talking about freshman initiation. He called it Freshman Frenzy.

I groaned.

"Several students have already been caught—upperclassmen, of course—for stealing clothes during PE." He smiled with kind, sympathetic eyes. "I thought it was wise to warn all of you—not to alarm anyone. Just be on the lookout."

I raised my hand. "What sort of initiation stunts should we watch for?"

He held his finger near his mouth. "Every year there are cases of books missing, kids being locked inside lockers, salt replaced for sugar in the cafeteria—things like that. Last year, however, someone nearly drowned when a dunking stunt got out of hand. We certainly don't want any of our freshmen to feel endangered." He paused, looking more serious now. "However, this sort of thing is usually done by mid-September, so be especially on the lookout during the next two weeks."

Later, after announcements were over, I was torn between answering Sean's letter and rewriting Andie's campaign speech. I sighed and stared out the window, feeling concern for Andie. The odds were stacked against her. I couldn't imagine any senior jumping on board with our idea. Shoot, if I were a senior, would I let initiation slip through my fingers?

It was impossible to jump ahead three years into the future and know for sure what I'd be thinking. Three years from now . . . let's see. I'd be starting my senior year, still getting top grades, hopefully, and being a person who would be willing to listen to a lowly freshman. And Sean? Would he still be in my life—writing great letters, maybe arranging to fly out and ski some weekends?

"Holly Meredith." Mr. Irving was calling my name.

I jerked to attention. "Uh . . . yes?"

"The principal would like to see you." He came down the row to my desk. "You're not in trouble," he assured me.

I knew that. People know when they're in trouble. I hoped no one was sick at home or anything. Quickly, I grabbed my backpack.

The office was not as crowded as I expected. Instead, it was populated by two secretaries and a couple of kids waiting to see the counselor.

I was talking to one of the secretaries when Mr. Crane came out of his private office. "You must be Holly Meredith." He extended his hand.

"Yes . . . hello." I shook his hand, feeling a little strange about this formality.

He led me into his office and pulled out a chair. I sat down, wondering what this was all about. Mr. Crane, my new principal, sat behind his wide desk. Then he leaned forward and folded his hands. "One of our student editors, Marcia Greene, has been telling me about you and your terrific writing," he began. "And it occurred to me that perhaps you'd be interested in befriending another writer—a new student. We've taken her under our collective wing, so to speak, mainly because she happens to be handicapped . . . blind."

I couldn't get a handle on any of this. Why was he talking to me?

Finally he made himself clear. "Marcia thinks you are a good choice for a part-time student aide for Tina Frazer."

I listened intently.

"Tina has a high academic rating and is being mainstreamed into regular classes as a four-week experiment. Are you interested in an assigned friendship?" He chuckled somewhat nervously.

A high academic rating . . . an assigned friendship. The whole thing sounded too impersonal. I remembered the pixie-haired girl I'd seen in the cafeteria. She'd seemed lonely; no one had talked to her that first day. "Does Tina know about the experiment?" I asked.

"As a matter of fact, she volunteered for it."

Now I was more interested, knowing that she wasn't being a guinea pig. "Did she attend the School for the Deaf and the Blind?" I asked.

"She's always been one of their top students," he explained. "But the school is becoming overcrowded as more handicapped students are moving here from Denver. Parents are concerned about big-city crime; they want to live in a quieter, less hectic place."

Dressel Hills was the ticket—an ideal place for families. I could see why parents with handicapped kids would choose to live here.

I was definitely interested in volunteering to be Tina's aide, but I wondered how tending to a blind student's needs would fit into my campaign plans with Andie.

Mr. Crane sensed my hesitation. "Think about it for a couple of days. In the meantime, Marcia will be assisting Tina."

I wondered why Marcia couldn't continue; then I remembered. She had more responsibility than ever, being on the student staff of the school paper.

I thanked the principal for thinking of me and headed back down the hall. That's when I spotted Tina Frazer and her wonderful dog. The two of them were waiting outside the nurse's office. Alone. Marcia Greene was nowhere in sight.

Not wanting to startle the girl, I scuffed my shoes across the floor as I approached her. "You're Tina, aren't you?"

She smiled. "That's right."

"My name is Holly Meredith. I'm glad to meet you."

Tina held out her hand and I shook it. "Thanks, it's nice to talk with someone who's not afraid to strike up a conversation."

I gazed at her beautiful guide dog. "What a gorgeous dog you have."

She nodded. "Everyone thinks so. Her name is Taffy and she adores people."

"I can see that." Then I realized what I'd said—about seeing—and instantly felt stupid.

The nurse opened the door and Tina turned to me. "I hope I'll see you again, Holly."

"Same here," I said, trying to deal with her usage of "see."

My walk back to homeroom was more leisurely than my wild pace had been minutes before—prior to meeting Tina. What a delightful person. I couldn't get over how outgoing she was. I guess I'd mistakenly pegged blind people as being shy and withdrawn. But Tina was very friendly. And that guide dog of hers—Taffy—what an amazing animal.

By the time I set foot in Mr. Irving's homeroom, I'd almost forgotten the problems Andie faced with her election campaign. Almost, but not entirely.

Lunch hour held the key.

The weather had turned warm by noon. As warm as any Indian summer I'd experienced this close to the Rocky Mountains. I suggested to Andie that we have our meeting with the seniors outside, but she had other ideas.

"We need to meet them on their own turf," she insisted.

"Are you sure?" I pleaded. "It feels like summer again."

"Relax, Holly. Let's do it my way for a change." There was an icy edge to her words.

Jared and Amy-Liz showed up. Together, naturally. But it was still weird seeing them as a couple.

Billy, Shauna, and Joy came into the cafeteria a few seconds later. Paula and Kayla seemed to want to hang around and be involved, too. Even though they had nothing at stake in this, Andie decided they should stay. "For moral support," she said. That was the first blow to my ego, and I should've seen what was coming.

Andie worked her charm with two senior boys from our church. They didn't care either way about curbing initiation. They just seemed jazzed to be seniors. Who wouldn't?

After they left, Andie and the rest of us headed across the cafeteria—to the back where the windows created a panoramic view. Zye Greene and a whole group of seniors sat waiting, most of them drinking soda from cans. Guess it wasn't cool for seniors to eat lunch (at least not in the presence of freshmen). Anyway, the upbeat aspect of things quickly dissolved.

Zye sat there like King Tut. His lips curled into a disdainful sneer. "Look . . . uh, Andrea, is it?"

Andie's face reddened, but not from embarrassment. She was mad. "C'mon, you know who I am."

Hang in there, Andie, I thought.

Zye leaned back in his chair and cracked his knuckles. "I think I'm beginning to see who you are." His fingers drummed the table impatiently.

Andie stood firm. "As you know, we were supposed to be in junior high this year." She glanced at all of us. "So if you really want to be cool about things, you'd realize that fairness is in order here. And you seniors are the ones to get the ball rolling."

Wow, was she bold!

I thought by the way Zye was unbuttoning his top shirt button that maybe he was getting hot under the collar. Andie, after all, was coming across like a pro.

"Fairness has never been a consideration in the past." Zye stood up. He reminded me of an Elvis impersonator with his black pants and boots and that leather bomber jacket.

"So are you saying there's no room to negotiate?" I heard Andie say.

"You're hearing it right, girl." Zye cracked his knuckles again.

"Well, that's really a shame," Andie said. "I can see we're not dealing with typical seniors here—seniors with *class*."

I thought she was pushing it and tugged on the back of her shirt. "Forget it," I whispered.

Another guy stood up. "Hey, you've got a lot of gall, talking that way. Don'tcha have no respect?"

Zye clicked his fingers and the other kid sat down. "This conversation's done. We're outta here," he said.

Good riddance, I thought. Not only was the guy an arrogant jerk, his friend needed grammar lessons.

"We tried," Andie said when it was over. And there we sat, a bunch of whipped freshmen too baffled to move. Zye and his entourage had exited loudly to the sitting area outside.

I stared out the huge cafeteria window at the students outside. Some of the senior girls were sunning themselves on the flagstone walkway. Others stood around talking and laughing with guys.

Zye sauntered around while sharing his soda with a blond cheerleader. Then I noticed a familiar figure approach him. Medium height, mousy brown hair . . .

I studied him. Then I called to Andie. "Hey, look who's hanging out with Zye." I pulled her over to the window.

"You're kidding," she whispered. "I thought Ryan Davis was history."

Ryan was either a junior or a senior, I didn't know which. I hadn't seen him around school until now. He had that know-it-all upperclassman attitude and a letter jacket that smacked of machismo.

I'd first met Ryan last summer when Stan brought him home for supper after a swim meet at the Y. Now, however, it looked as though Ryan was linked up with Zye. "And I thought that opposites attract!" I said a bit too loudly.

Paula and Kayla came rushing over. "What's going on?" Paula asked as the twins peered out at the gruesome twosome.

Kayla clutched her throat. "Oh, say it isn't so."

"I knew that Zye fellow reminded me of someone," Paula interjected.

"Right," I agreed, hoping the thing between Zye and the freshman delegation had nothing to do with the color of Andie's skin. Ryan had slung some disgusting racial slurs at Andie last summer.

"This is *so* sick," Andie said, staring at Ryan.

"Don't let it freak you out, about Ryan, I mean. We both know what he's about."

"He's prejudiced," she persisted.

I wanted to change the subject, to get Andie's mind off what had happened between her and Ryan last summer. "Look, I'm proud of you." I touched her shoulder. "You handled things really well just now."

"Thanks," she said, sounding discouraged.

"You did your best and that's what counts," Paula said, trying to cheer her up.

♥　♥　♥

After school, Billy Hill stopped by my locker. "Did you think up any clever sayings for my campaign?"

"Yep." I pulled out my notebook. "Here you go. Billy Hill's No Hillbilly—Vote for a CLASS Act—Class Treasurer."

He grinned. "That's cool. Thanks, Holly."

"Any time." I closed my locker.

"Man, we need some decent leadership around here," he said. "After the way those seniors acted today at lunch . . ."

"I know what you mean."

"So . . ." He seemed hesitant. "I thought maybe you could write up something about me in *The Summit*. You know, just a blip on an unknown freshman running for office."

"I'd love to, Billy. It's just that I'm not officially on the paper staff yet." I didn't want to tell him about Marcia's comments about having me write an occasional piece for the paper. Mainly because I was still wondering how complicated it would be to juggle everything. Grades came first.

Billy shrugged his shoulders. "Oh well, I thought it wouldn't hurt to ask." He turned to leave.

"Billy!" I grabbed his arm. "Don't get the wrong idea. I'll gladly campaign for you. Hey, we want to see how many Christian kids we can get into office, right?"

"Thanks." He smiled broadly. "That'll be cool."

"Want me to nominate you tomorrow?" I asked as he waited for me to get my books.

"Actually, Paula already offered. Thanks anyway."

"Okay."

"Maybe you should be the one to nominate *Andie*, since she's your best friend," he suggested just as Paula came walking over.

"Oh, I'm planning to," I said, all smiles.

Paula shook her head. "Too late. It's already set."

"What is?" I asked.

"Amy-Liz is nominating Andie at your class meeting tomorrow," she said rather haughtily.

I frowned. "But she's running for secretary, right?"

Paula nodded confidently, like she was aware of other privileged information.

"I don't get it." I tried to suppress the hurt.

"Well, I'm sure you understand the saying 'one good turn deserves another'?"

I hadn't the faintest clue what she was getting at. "What's that got to do with this?"

"Plenty. Andie's nominating Amy-Liz." And with that, she and Billy left to catch the bus.

I stood there gasping. Why did it seem that every time I turned my back, Andie had conducted some private meeting? Without me.

14

Monday, September 9
Dear Sean,

I got your letter two days ago. It was interesting, especially the part about your wanting me to decide about your hair! Please feel free to do absolutely anything you want to. I'm thinking of doing something different with my newly permed hair, too. Something to get rid of all these curls!

How's your calculus teacher, Mr. Fremont? I'm sorry to hear about his cancer. Does he have pain? I always worry when I hear that someone has cancer. My favorite aunt died from it about two years ago. She was too young to die—around my mom's age. Anyway, I'll be praying for your teacher.

So much has happened since I wrote you last. Remember all those initiation questions I had? Well, this year it's come down from the top (seniors, of course!) that there's going to be fierce initiation. But, lowly freshmen that we are, we've decided that the sophomores are the ones who really deserve it.

I went on to explain how the sophomores of Dressel Hills High had experienced last year what we were missing now—top of the heap. So in our minds, that meant we shouldn't be punished twice. It made perfect sense!

> *About the grading scale here, we have the same as you do. I can't get used to a 94% being a high B— it's six points away from 100, for pete's sake!*
>
> *Andie's running for president of the freshman class. She wants me to write her campaign speech, and I promised I would, but now . . .*

I read the last two sentences and decided not to tell Sean about Andie's and my differences. I used white correction fluid to cover my words and rewrote the last sentence.

> *She's turning into a regular social bug. It was unbelievable how she handled herself today at lunch with some of the world's worst egomaniacs ever! Stay tuned . . .*
>
> *I met an interesting girl today. Her name is Tina Frazer, blind from birth. She's here for an experiment—mainstreaming a handicapped student—and I personally hope it's going to be successful.*
>
> *Well, I have lots of homework tonight, so I'd better end this letter.*

I paused before I signed off, wondering if I should follow his lead. Sean always signed "Yours," which could be taken several ways. Of course, he wasn't really mine, that wasn't what this was about.

Sean and I had a very long, very interesting conversation last summer about the boy-girl thing. And I was pleased in the end how we managed to agree to be friends. Even though Sean had asked me out while I was in California, I think he realized that a long-distance romance really wasn't possible. Not at our age.

So the way I signed my letters must not encourage him toward anything but continuing the correspondence the way we'd started. When it came right down to it, I was enjoying this sort of friendship with a guy. Sean had never been pushy, and I liked the fact that he seemed to want me to decide things, too.

The age difference was a minor factor in all this. In five years it wouldn't matter, though. I'd be nineteen going on twenty and he'd be twenty-one. For now, things were best the way they were.

I slid Goofey, my cat, off my lap and settled him gently onto the window seat where the two of us curled up together. Reading, writing, list-making, and praying—all this was most readily carried out when I was cocooned away in my window-seat alcove. A world apart.

I signed my letter "Your friend" and addressed the envelope. Then I ran all the way down to the mailbox, beating the late pickup by only a few seconds.

Back at home, I gathered up two loads of my laundry and headed downstairs. Laundry was one of my weekday chores, so I'd designated Monday as my wash day.

I thought of Andie slaving over her washing machine as a future mother, churning out one load of wash after another. All those children . . .

"Holly!" called Stan from the family room.

I peeked my head around the corner. "That's my name, don't wear it out!"

"Grow up," he muttered.

"What do you want?"

"Uh . . . just wondered. What's with Andie running for freshman class president?"

"It's a free country, you know."

"But isn't it a little out of character for her?" He looked like a toad, all scrunched up on the floor in front of the sofa behind the coffee table. Cracking pecans.

I stared. "What are you doing?"

"Mom's baking, and I'm helping out."

"Oh." This was a first.

"So . . . what's up with Andie?" He was holding the nutcracker in midair.

"Is there an echo in here?" I looked around. "For your information, Andie's emerging from her junior-high shell."

He sighed. "Then what's she doing talking to a bunch of upperclassmen?"

"She has an important agenda, that's what." I disappeared behind the laundry room door. It would be only a few seconds before Stan burst in here making demands.

"Well," Stan said, barging right in, "your friend's making herself way too visible."

I tossed the whites into the washing machine

and started the water. "Yeah, well, none of us would be normal if we didn't change a little as we mature. Isn't that what Mom's always saying—Uncle Jack, too—that we have to be flexible in order to grow up?"

He glared at me. It was obvious he didn't want solid answers. "Andie's getting way too popular for her own good."

"You're just jealous."

He cocked his blond head. "Jealous of what?"

"You know . . ."

He blew air through his lips in disgust. "Hey, guess what Zye Greene thinks?" he said, surprising me with his sudden reference to Marcia's brother.

"Who cares what Zye-in-your-eye thinks, so don't waste your breath!"

Stan frowned and ran his fingers through his hair. "He liked her," he said in a half whisper. "He—"

"That's hard to believe. If he liked her so much, why was he such a jerk today?" I interrupted and poured the liquid detergent over the laundry and shut the lid. "Now, if you'll excuse me, I have homework coming out of my ears."

I shoved past him.

"Holly, wait!" He grabbed my shirttail. "Do you think she's . . . uh, getting in a little over her head?"

I had no idea what this brousin of mine was mumbling. "Look, if you want to catch all the latest on your ex-girlfriend, why don't you just give her a call?"

He actually slumped against the furnace. "You don't get it, do you?"

"You're right, I don't." And with that I headed upstairs.

Later, while I was eyebrow-deep in algebra, Andie called. Only I didn't talk to her. I asked Mom to tell her I'd see her tomorrow at school. Hopefully she'd understand. This homework thing was unreal.

♥ ♥ ♥

The next morning in homeroom, after announcements, the freshman class was dismissed and we poured into the school auditorium. There were kids with posters and banners everywhere. And Andie came in carrying a large flag that read "Andie's a Dandy!"

Did she come up with the clever slogan on her own? I finally got Andie's attention and squeezed past three kids to the empty seat next to her.

"This is going to be so cool." She held the homemade flag on her lap, wriggling with anticipation. "See what we made?" she said, showing me the flag.

I glanced at the flag, guessing who "we" was and deciding not to comment. I wanted this moment to be special between us. Squelching the feeling to probe, I settled back and waited for the assembly to begin.

Andie looked rather peachy—I mean her cheeks. I didn't want to stare, but it seemed she was wearing more makeup than usual. And a sharp new outfit: designer jeans and a black sweater jacket over a white shirt.

"Hey, fabulous clothes," I said, touching the sleeve of her new sweater.

"Dad finally broke down and let me buy something new just for today." She was wired up. Had on new perfume.

"Lucky you," I said, smiling.

"I called you last night . . . to tell you about it."

"Sorry," I said. "I had tons of homework."

"That's what your mom said." There was a ring of accusation in her voice.

Then two boys behind us started the clapping as the high-school principal, Mr. Crane, stood up to the podium. For a moment I felt a twinge of sadness for my old school. My junior-high days— the good old days—before algebra and homework to the hilt.

Mr. Crane got things rolling. And soon Amy-Liz was on her feet. "I would like to nominate Andrea Martinez for freshman class president."

Explosive applause. And whistling.

Andie stood and waved to her fans with absolute style. She beamed her thanks, and I watched my dearest friend as she seemed to metamorphose before my eyes. Andie's poise and confidence surprised me.

I pinched myself to make sure I wasn't dreaming, and then a girl three rows away stood up and made the nomination for Jeff Kinney. I turned my attention away from Andie, who was talking with kids behind us, pretty much ignoring me. The sights and sounds muddled together, and I noticed Amy-Liz standing up again, proudly nominating Jared for vice president.

Andie kept bumping into me, like she didn't even know I was there. She was so caught up with the moment—bustling in and out of her seat, chatting with everyone around her. The worst part happened right on the heels of the assembly. I wanted to hug Andie and give her my support—tell her how thrilled I was at the response of the students. But she and I somehow became separated in the crush of students while exiting the auditorium.

To make matters worse, Paula and Kayla were waiting in the hallway. I could see them just ahead of me. A lump jammed in my throat as my best friend literally ran to the twins with the swell of the crowd at her back.

By the time I was able to forge through the flood, Andie and the Miller twins had vanished.

15

With tears threatening to spill over, I headed for the girls' rest room and into one of the stalls. I dabbed some toilet paper at my eyes, careful not to smudge my mascara.

What right had Paula and Kayla to intercept Andie and snatch her away from me? We were all friends, for pete's sake!

Frantic feelings, similar to the ones I'd had on the first day of high school, enveloped me. I stood inside the bathroom stall clinging to my books, fighting back tears.

That's when I heard Andie's voice trickle into the rest room, followed by the jovial sounds of Paula and Kayla. The three of them were laughing, having a fabulous time while I hid, my face all streaked with tears.

Andie began to replay the class meeting for the twins' benefit. I could almost see them touching up their hair and makeup as Andie chattered on. "I couldn't believe how everyone clapped when Amy-Liz nominated me."

"Oh, I can believe it," Paula said, pouring it on. "You're going to make a wonderful class president."

Kayla spoke up. "Why did you wait so long to call us last night? We were absolutely thrilled to drop everything and come help with your banners and flags."

Paula continued. "It's really unfortunate about Holly. After all, she was your first choice."

"Right," Andie said. "Before school ever started she promised to be my campaign manager, and now this."

I frowned, feeling caged in. No one was making any sense! What did she mean—"now this"?

"Do you think Holly's using her homework as an excuse?" Kayla said.

Andie was silent.

Paula cut in. "I don't think she would do that. But then, Andie knows her better than we do."

"Does *anyone* know what's going on with Holly Meredith this year?" Kayla asked. "She's certainly not herself, if you know what I mean."

"Yeah," Andie was finally talking. "I hate to say it, but I think she's jealous about the election thing. To tell you the truth, I think she's ticked because she isn't running for student council herself."

I despised what I was hearing and wanted to shout, "You're wrong—all of you!" but I remained silent, hoping the three of them would leave. The sooner, the better.

Angrily I stared at the graffiti scribbled on the door in front of my eyes, wishing I could block the sound of senseless chatter from my friends.

When Andie and the twins finally left, I reached for the latch. It was jammed!

"Hey, let me out!" I called.

There were snickers, unrecognizable ones. Then a scurry to the door, and silence.

I leaped up on the toilet seat and looked out over the door. No one was around. A message in red lipstick danced across the mirror. Freshman Frenzy!

I groaned and had to crawl out of the stall on my hands and knees. Quickly, I brushed myself off and washed my hands. Checking my hair, I realized that the perm was weakening a bit—getting more manageable every day. In fact, I was sure that by tomorrow I could wear my hair down instead of covering it with a baseball cap. Thank goodness for small miracles!

I knew the bell for second hour was about to ring, so I hurried through the motions of touching up my makeup and getting myself together emotionally. Could I manage my second-period class—choir—without breaking down again? I cleared my throat and tried to hum as I pushed the door open and raced to my locker. Who could sing at a time like this?

I ran all the way up the stairs to the choir room, and just as I was rounding the corner, I spied

Marcia Greene walking alongside Tina Frazer and her dog, Taffy.

"Marcia, Tina . . . hey!" I called.

"It's Holly," Tina said, smiling.

"How'd you know?" I said.

Tina laughed. "I depend on my hearing to identify people. That . . . and smells."

"Well, then, it's a good thing I showered this morning," I teased.

Marcia seemed happy to see me. But Tina was the one doing the talking. "Are you headed for choir?" Tina asked.

"Sure am." Glancing at Marcia, I volunteered to take Tina to choir.

Marcia smiled pleasantly. "That'd be great, Holly. Thanks." I held my right arm out for Tina, the way I'd seen Marcia do. Tina wove her left arm into mine and we headed down the hall. "How's school so far?" I asked.

"Oh, it's the best," she said. "And I love choir."

"Me too. Especially four-part harmony," I commented. "Just wait'll we get into Christmas music."

"I can't wait." Tina's face shone with joy. "May I sit with you?"

"That'd be great." I thought about the prospect of having a blind choral partner.

"I promise not to sing off-key. I really do have a good ear." She laughed softly, and I opened the door to the music room.

The bell rang just as we found two seats

together in the soprano section. Two rows away, Andie was accompanied on both sides by Paula and Kayla. It was obvious to me she didn't want me to join them. Not a single chair in sight.

I focused my attention on the director and the new a cappella madrigal in our folders. And on Tina Frazer—a girl with a spirit of peace. Blindness was not a hindrance to her well-being. I sensed it in the way she spoke to me. The way she carried herself. The way she sat tall in her choir chair. Confidence was her middle name.

Once again, I felt ashamed.

♥ ♥ ♥

After school there were posters popping up everywhere. Zillions of them. The "Andie's a Dandy" slogan showed up on bright red banners mounted high on the walls. Above the row of freshman lockers. High on the arched doors leading to the gymnasium. In the girls' locker room downstairs. I'd even noticed one in the shower during seventh-hour PE.

Andie and the Miller twins had probably posted them during lunch. I was sure they would use the excuse that I was nowhere to be found, which was true. Evidently they hadn't waited for me. Not at all.

Feeling deserted, I'd run off to the Soda Straw three blocks away for a burger and a strawberry shake. A place to think, to get lost in the crowd. While there, I'd made a list of pros and cons, deciding whether or not I actually had time to be assigned to Tina. An intriguing person—and a magnetic personality. Even if I had wanted to resist, my curiosity drew me to her.

Yet, interesting as Tina was, she made no demands on me. Which was perfectly refreshing in contrast to the way things were turning out between Andie and me. I couldn't even do my homework (and not answer the phone for once in my life) without Andie jumping to all sorts of conclusions. And the Miller-twin thing was really getting out of hand. Shoot, they were running everything. Andie's campaign included.

So . . . I guess the bottom line was that I just felt left out. But there was someone for me—a girl who could graciously accept my help, who had a way of brightening up the world around her. Tina—a blind girl with a laugh and a sparkle always gracing her face.

♥   ♥   ♥

The bus ride home was not only lonely, it was tiresome. Noisy, too. With so many high-school students taking the city bus, it seemed as though we'd never get to Downhill Court. And try as I might, I couldn't stop thinking about the fact that Andie wasn't there.

I thought back to the morning assembly. Andie, in all her glory, had accepted the rousing applause gracefully yet eagerly. My heavyhearted feelings returned as I remembered Amy-Liz standing and nominating my closest friend. Not a pretty picture. I should've been the one standing up, proudly nominating Andie Martinez. Sure, I was probably blowing things out of proportion, but I couldn't do things any other way.

When I arrived home, Mom had a plate of snickerdoodles waiting in the kitchen. "How was your day, Holly-Heart?"

"The worst."

She glanced at me. "Want to talk about it?"

"Not now." I reached for two cookies. "Probably never."

She frowned, going back to the sink, where she washed the cookie sheets and the mixing bowl. I went to the refrigerator and poured a tall glass of milk. Nothing in the world goes better with snickerdoodles than a cold glass of milk. Nothing, except maybe your friends hanging out with you, sharing your favorite snack.

I knocked that thought out of my consciousness. "Mom," I asked, "did you have lots of friends in school . . . or only one?"

She turned to look at me for a second, then dried her hands. "I was always one for having a few close friends, I guess." Mom stayed near the sink, leaning against the counter. "I can count on one hand the best friends I had in school."

I took a long drink of milk.

"Why do you ask?" I figured that was coming. Mom knew me well. She and I could pretty much predict each other's moods as well as thoughts.

"Just wondered," I muttered into my milk.

She wouldn't let it go at that; I was sure of it. And she didn't. "It's not easy moving into a new era of your life, honey." With those gentle words, she got me talking.

"But it's so cruel out there," I said. "I think I've been spoiled, you know?" I hated it when squeaks came instead of my normal voice. A dead giveaway to loss of emotional control.

But Mom was cool. She acted like I was totally together. "Some people have many good, close friends—they'd probably refer to a casual acquaintance as a very dear friend. Your stepdad is like that. He's an extrovert—has oodles of friends."

I smiled, thinking of Uncle Jack's charming ways. "I know what you mean. But what about my personality? Why'd I have to get stuck being an introvert?"

Mom's eyebrows arched slightly. "I wouldn't call you an introvert, exactly. None of us is simply one thing or another. There are many combinations and blends of personality traits."

"Then what about Uncle Jack; you just said he—"

"Your stepdad seems to be rather gregarious out in public," she explained, "and also when interacting with you kids. But there are times when he likes to be quiet and relax with absolutely no one around."

"Not even you?" This was a surprise.

She smiled. "Not even me."

I sighed. "So, then, what am I?"

Mom came over to the bar and sat on a stool. Her timing was perfect. I wasn't threatened by her being close now. In fact, I needed her near. She began again softly. "Years ago, when you were a toddler, I read a book about this very thing. I wasn't a Christian back then, but I understood in some small way that God had created each of us with a myriad of characteristics which, together, make up our personalities."

I listened, fascinated. Never had I heard Mom talk about this.

"You have a high-spirited temperament, Holly," she continued. "But you are also loyal and patient. Often you suffer in silence instead of lashing out."

"Unless it involves my family," I said, remembering how I fought to visit Daddy two summers ago.

Mom agreed. "Ever notice how you enjoy spending time in your room, writing in your journal . . . contemplating life?"

I nodded. "It feels good being alone sometimes."

"Well, some people derive energy from being alone. Others need to be around people in order to feel charged up—alive."

I was starting to get the picture. "I think Andie's one of those people types," I said without thinking.

"So is your father."

"Carrie, too?" I asked.

She nodded. "And Stephie, although I haven't completely figured her out yet." Mom chuckled.

"What happens when two friends have opposite personalities?" I figured Mom knew what I was really getting at.

"I think that's probably a good sign. Some of the best friendships of history came out of personality contrasts."

"Give me an example." I was dying to know.

"Well, one comes to mind without trying too hard—David and Jonathan," she said. "David was an outgoing, gregarious warrior, and Jonathan was a loyal, behind-the-scenes kind of guy."

I was beginning to see that maybe Andie and I just needed some time apart. Maybe if she hung around the Miller twins long enough, she'd get tired and come home. To me.

Mom continued, "Sometimes, though—and you may already know this—people drift apart during the high-school years. It has much to do with growing up—finding who you are. That's not to say that your closest friends won't always be special to you; they will, but many times your circle of friends begins to widen from mid- and late-teens on. It's a normal outgrowth of maturity."

What a blow! Mom had just implied that if I were mature enough, I'd be moving ahead with my life, with or without Andie. How could she say such a thing? I mulled things over in silence.

"Holly?" She leaned over and touched my hair.

I didn't want to hurt her. My negative reaction would have to stay well hidden. "I think it's time to write in my journal," I said, carrying my glass over to the sink. "My energy is fading, if you know what I mean."

She nodded, catching on.

I ran up the stairs and exploded into my bedroom. So much for suffering in silence!

16

After supper, when my homework was finished and Mom had signed all my paper work for school, I made campaign buttons for Billy. An athletic student from way back in grade school, Billy was excited to include student politics in his life. And to be the freshman class treasurer was a nice addition to his high-school resumé.

Stan sauntered through the kitchen at one point, stopped, and peered over my shoulder at the campaign buttons. "Who in the world would wear those?" he said, then left.

I ignored his snide remark, wondering how I'd survive when he started dishing out freshman initiation. Initiation had been referred to as many things, some names worse than others, but the word was out—there would never be another year like this one. Already it was beginning. I knew they'd never be satisfied with merely locking *one* freshman in a bathroom stall. No way.

Mark, Phil, Carrie, and Stephie emerged from the family room and hung around to watch me work. When the boys finally wandered off to do homework at Uncle Jack's nudging, I waited for Carrie and Stephie to do the same.

"Don't you two have something to do?" I asked.

"We never get homework," Carrie said.

"Wish I were back in grade school," I muttered.

The girls were eager to help. I could tell by the anguished looks on their little faces. And being the wise big sister, I knew they'd never stop pleading until I gave them each a pair of scissors. "Make sure you cut perfect circles so the labels will fit into the plastic button holders."

"We will—we know how to cut," Carrie insisted.

"Yeah, we're pros," Stephie said.

Mom, observing the situation, grinned at me. "How are things going with Andie's campaign?"

I really didn't want to talk about that. "She's doing okay, I guess. The students went wild at our class meeting this morning."

"Oh?" Mom raised her eyebrows, showing definite interest. "Is that because my Holly-Heart has been busy pulling things together for her?"

"If you mean have I been out there organizing Andie's election, the answer is no."

Carrie and Stephie stared at me. "Ew, she's mad," I heard Stephie whisper.

"You bet I am!"

Stephie inched away from the bar and blinked her long eyelashes.

Mom frowned. "Holly, please."

I looked at the youngest of our blended family. "Sorry," I whispered. Then, turning to Mom, I cut loose. "Honestly? Andie's making me crazy. She starts out literally begging me to help her, appoints me as her campaign chairman and all that, and pleads with me to write her speech."

Mom looked puzzled. "Then what?"

"She gets all bent out of shape because I don't talk to her last night—remember when she called?—I was doing my algebra."

Mom nodded, watching me intently.

"Then today, she has the nerve to act like I don't exist." I paused, catching my breath. "You should've heard Andie and the Miller twins going off about me."

"How'd that happen?" Mom leaned on the kitchen bar.

"Well, they sauntered into the rest room and started shooting off all these theories they had about me. It was so bizarre."

"And where were you?" asked Mom.

"Locked in one of the stalls," I said, explaining that some hotsy-totsy upperclassmen had chosen that moment to crank up the wheels of initiation.

"You're angry, Holly."

Mom was right, but I couldn't speak. Not now.

She sighed. "Is that why you're helping Billy and not Andie?"

Tears welled up and I fought them back.

Carrie and Stephie were hard at work making perfect circles. They seemed disinterested, which was a relief. Mom, however, motioned me out of the kitchen. "Little squeakers have big ears," she whispered as we headed for the living room.

On the way, I glanced back at the girls. "You asked about Andie and that's what's happening."

Mom sat on the sofa. She seemed eager to talk to me in private. "I wonder," she said, "have you thought about all of this from Andie's perspective?"

I leaned forward on the rocker. "I've tried. Maybe not very hard, though."

"Is it possible that you've been acting a bit selfishly in all of this?"

I leaned against the rocker, thinking back over the past few days. I'd been possessive of Andie, disagreeable, too. No wonder Andie felt the way she did. Still, I couldn't relinquish my anger.

The rocker creaked rhythmically as Mom stared at me.

"Why don't you pray about this?" she suggested at last.

I could feel my heels digging in. Stubbornly, I shrugged. "Maybe later."

Mom picked up a magazine, concern still imprinted on her face. I headed for the kitchen to finish up Billy's campaign buttons.

Later, when everything was cleaned up, I went to my room. I knew if I wrote in my journal before calling Andie, it would take some of the fire out of my words. Something a non-extrovert would probably do.

I located my journal in the bottom drawer of my dresser. Then, since it was almost dark outside, I sat at my desk.

Tuesday, September 10: I wish I knew what was happening between Andie and me. She's so strange these days—which is something she said about me earlier today as I innocently eavesdropped on her.

All this talk about Paula and Kayla promoting Andie is really bugging me. They're sophomores! I still can see Andie rushing to them after the class meeting this morning. It was actually cruel! I mean, there I was sitting right beside her and she didn't even have the courtesy to turn around and share her exhilaration. How could she do this to me?

I stopped and scanned the page, rereading my entry. Was I overreacting?

I continued to write.

Mom and I had a talk today after school. She gave me some insight into my own personality. I've been enlightened. (Ha!) But I'm going to check out some library books and thoroughly analyze myself anyway.

Mom says I should be praying about my disagreeable self. That hurts.

I closed my journal and set it aside. Leaning back in my chair, I stared at my lavender-and-white bedroom. The canopy over my bed had been cleaned last spring and it was starting to look a bit dusty.

Funny. When you've spent practically your whole life in the same room, everything around you feels solid. The same way the most comfortable relationships feel. I thought of Andie. Paula, too. Was I ready to let them go—move forward—to broaden my circle of friends?

Life without my two best friends . . . Sure sounded like a good title for a sad book. Maybe I'd write something like that someday. And when I was all grown up, and the pain of this week had long since dimmed—when I needed a point of reference—I would return to this journal and reread the trauma of the first horrible week of my freshman year.

The entries concerning Andie and me, the way I felt wounded over being left out, all of it, would refresh my memory. Maybe the book would be for teen girls. Yeah, that's what I would do. Someday . . .

I got up and put my journal away. Then I went to the hall and leaned over the long banister. The house was quiet. Maybe, just maybe, the portable phone was free. It was time for a heart-to-heart talk with Andie.

17

Andie picked up on the third ring.

"Hey," I said, hesitantly. "Guess who?"

"I'm busy," she said.

"Homework?"

"You could say that." There were giggles in the background.

My heart was in my throat. "You're working on your campaign, right?"

"Kinda."

I waited, hoping she'd invite me over. When she didn't, I felt dizzy, like I was going to black out.

"You still there, Holly?"

"Uh . . . I guess so."

"What's wrong?" she asked, amidst a backdrop of fun and friends.

"I just called to tell you how happy I am about today."

"Well, if I win, it's no thanks to you. You haven't done much of anything."

The anger rose in me. Mom had said that I often simmered in silence. But right now I felt like a volcano about to erupt.

"You don't have time for me anymore." Her words were like ice. "Your homework and other things, like making campaign buttons for Billy Hill, are much more important these days, right?"

How'd she know about the buttons for Billy? I wondered.

She kept going, and finally I couldn't take it any longer. "Just stop, Andie. Stop right now," I hollered into the phone. "I've had it with you and those secret meetings you never invite me to. If you want to do everything on your own without help from me, then fine. And while you're at it, go ahead and write your own campaign speech!" There, I'd said it.

And then it happened. Without a single word of protest, without Andie pleading with me to rethink things, I heard the sound that echoed in my memory for days to come.

Click. She'd hung up the phone!

I beeped off the cordless phone and curled up on my bed. Goofey must've sensed my sadness. He came padding over and jumped onto the bed. Gently, I put my head against his soft body and let his purring soothe me.

Crying, I began to pray. "Oh, Lord, what's wrong with me? Is Mom right? Am I the one who made things go all wrong with Andie?" I sobbed into my pillow. "Please help me. I feel so sad. My best friend just turned her back on me. She didn't even argue with me at the end. What does it mean, Lord?"

I fell asleep with Goofey beside me. And later, around midnight, I realized Mom had come in and tried to tuck me in. There was only one problem with that, and it had nothing to do with falling asleep without my pajamas. Far worse—I hadn't finished my homework.

Drowsy, but awake enough to know it was now or never, I dragged myself out of bed. (Not being a morning person would spell disaster for a foggy thinker if I left it until 6:00 A.M.!)

So I began, working my algebra problems and then conjugating French verbs till nearly one o'clock. The fact that I'd already slept for several hours actually helped expedite things mentally, and by the time I was satisfied with my work, I was more than wide awake.

Reaching for my Marty Leigh mystery book, I stayed up for another thirty minutes, once again relishing the idea of being awake while the entire household snoozed away.

A week ago I'd done the same thing. Stayed up till the wee hours. Thank goodness my hair disaster was nearly over. I could cross off the frizzies on my list of prayer requests. And maybe, just maybe, Mom would agree to let me get my hair cut professionally, with layers to frame my face. What a great look that would be. And besides, I was honestly tired of long hair—it is too immature-looking for a freshman in high school!

Just before I turned out the lights, I undid my

French braid, surveying the situation. Yep. This weekend I would make an appointment at the beauty salon and see what could be done. Meanwhile, a good shampoo, a gentle blow-dry, and the hot styling brush was all I would need to create a glamorous high-school look for tomorrow. As glamorous as any freshman who'd ever darkened the halls of Dressel Hills High.

With that thought, I sprang into bed.

18

I couldn't remember ever getting the kind of stares I got while walking to my locker the next day. Even Mr. Irving complimented me on my hair as I strolled into homeroom. Even so, I still wanted to get a shorter, layered cut, so popular now.

Between classes, the halls buzzed with kids campaigning for each other. I, however, steered clear of Andie and her throng, which, surprisingly enough, now included Jared and Amy-Liz. I figured they'd be quite a clique if all of them got elected to student council.

To keep my mind off the sting in my heart, I busied myself with other things. Like taking good notes in all my classes and listening carefully to Jeff Kinney's campaign promises.

He strolled up to me unexpectedly during lunch period. Actually, it was before I even went to lunch. I was rummaging around in my locker when he stopped by, more friendly than ever.

"Hey, Holly. How's it going?" His eyes scanned my hair.

"Okay." I smiled, glad to have my hair down again and feeling like a zillion bucks—hair-wise. "Hey, sounds like you've got some great plans for the year."

"Yeah, all the soda you can drink on Fridays." His eyes held my gaze only for a moment, then awkwardly shifted away.

"That's a lot," I said, questioning him. "Who's paying for it?"

He turned squirmy on me and said he had to meet someone for lunch. "Don't forget—don't be a ninny . . ."

And he was off. Voting for Jeff Kinney was probably the dumbest thing a freshman could ever do. I was convinced the kid had no substance. Probably no access to lots of soda, either. I don't know why that occurred to me, but I had a strange feeling about his shifty eyes.

I decided to do some checking, starting with Mark Jones, Jeff's main sidekick. I waited at his locker.

"Hey," Mark said enthusiastically when he spotted me. "Your hair looks great."

"Thanks."

"You're going to vote for Jeff, right?" He flicked through his combination and opened his locker.

"Haven't decided," I said.

He turned and looked at me. "Well, you're not one of those bottled-water-only girls, are you?"

I laughed. "Not me, I love a good root beer."

"So what's the problem?" He folded his arms across his chest, moving closer. Uncomfortably close.

I realized then that he was flirting. I stepped back.

"I'm thinking of having a party next weekend and wondered if Jeff might be able to get me a deal on some soda." This wasn't a lie at all; I had seriously thought of throwing a party. A two-person party. For Tina and me.

Mark shook his head. "Out of the question. Jeff's dad is on company business."

"Oh," I said, picking up on something else. Something quite strange. Not only was Jeff Kinney unable to make eye contact and keep it, his best friend seemed to be having the same problem.

"Well, catch you later," he said.

I hurried to the cafeteria and got in the hot-lunch line. While waiting for a patty melt, I spotted Tina sitting back near the windows—the section designated by the seniors as their turf. I wondered if Tina knew she was trespassing. But then I remembered Taffy accompanied her everywhere. No way would Zye Greene or any other senior mess with a guide dog.

I paid for my lunch and headed toward Tina, passing right by Andie, who sat chattering at a table with the Miller twins, Jared, and Amy-Liz. None of them seemed to notice. And I refused to care.

Cautiously, I approached the blind girl's table.

"Hey, Tina," I said, holding my tray. "Mind if I join you?"

"Oh, Holly, it's you." She slid over. "Of course, have a seat."

I glanced down at Taffy, who was snoozing. "Your dog's having a nice nap."

"I could use one myself," she said. There was that charming laughter again. "Of course, no one would ever have to know, right? If I didn't close my eyes, I mean."

"That's an advantage to being blind, I suppose." I hoped my comment didn't sound too ridiculous.

Leaning back against the chair, I enjoyed the sun on my back. I was trying too hard—needed to be myself. But more than anything, I needed a friend.

"There are many benefits to being blind," Tina said, catching me off guard. "Most people wouldn't believe it, but I can actually hear better than a sighted person."

"Really? I thought your keen sense of hearing must have come from having to compensate for not seeing." I'd read that somewhere.

"Well, it definitely came in handy today." She leaned toward me. "I can give you some handy information; that is, if you're interested in not voting for Jeff Kinney."

Now I was curious. "Like what?"

Tina's face burst into an enormous grin. "Jeff's father is not a soda dealer, not even close."

"You're kidding!"

"He's a doctor," she stated.

"Are you sure?"

"Absolutely." She was still smiling. "Like I said, my hearing is one of my keenest senses."

I couldn't help myself. I danced in my seat. "This is too good to be true."

"So . . . who's going to start spreading the truth about him?" she asked.

"I, for one." Then I caught myself. Why was I so happy? Andie's election could possibly rest on whether or not I spread the word. If I really wanted to hurt her—get back at her—I'd keep Tina's secret to myself. Let Jeff win the vote.

Silence sliced the air.

"Something wrong, Holly?"

This girl was amazing. "Do you have a sixth sense or something?" I stared at her.

"Some people say that, but . . ." She paused for a moment. "Well, it's a long story. I wrote about it once. You're a writer, too, aren't you?"

"Marcia told you?"

She nodded. "But there's something she didn't tell me," Tina said.

Even though I knew Tina couldn't see me with her eyes, I felt as though she could see into my heart somehow. "What?" I managed to say. "What didn't Marcia tell you?"

Her words came softly. "That you needed a friend."

I swallowed the lump in my throat. "That's not all," I said, feeling more confident. "I've decided to be your student aide. Part time, full time . . .

whatever. I'll be at your beck and call."

"Who needs an aide?" Tina joked. "But if you want to hang with me, that'll be cool."

She was the cool one!

19

On the way to the principal's office, Andie and the Miller twins bumped into us. Well, not really collided or anything, but they noticed me walking with Tina. And they were scowling!

Andie and company were polite enough not to say anything rude, but if looks are the unspoken expression of the soul, I knew exactly what they were thinking.

"Hey, everyone," I said, remembering how Andie had hung up on me last night. Her eyes grew bigger with each step Tina and I took together. She was staring at Tina!

"Uh . . . hey yourself," Andie answered, and I noticed her braces. She must have gotten them yesterday and never told me. Andie fumbled in her backpack, probably an excuse so she wouldn't have to look at me.

Paula started to come over, but Kayla grabbed her arm and pulled her back, and the group abruptly turned and walked away. Instantly, I felt sad for Tina. Glad, too. Glad that Tina hadn't seen what I'd just witnessed. She was right; there *were* advantages to being blind.

Tina whispered, "Aren't you going to tell your friends about Jeff's dad being a doctor . . . not a soda-pop guy? How about that false campaign promise?"

"Later," I said. But in my heart, I wasn't so sure.

Not anymore.

♥   ♥   ♥

After my visit with the principal, I got Tina and Taffy settled into pre-algebra class. Then, with a note in hand signed by the principal informing my teachers of my new status of student aide, I hurried off to fifth period.

Mr. Irving stood behind his desk and greeted me in French as I came in. Quickly, I responded with the appropriate dialogue, thankful that I'd conjugated those verbs late last night.

He scanned the note I handed to him from the principal. "What a terrific thing to do, Holly," he said. I knew by the tone of his voice he meant it.

Unfortunately, my former friends, namely Andie, Paula, and Kayla, didn't seem to think my becoming an aide for a blind student was so terrific. I mean, as close as Andie and I had been for all our growing-up years, I never dreamed she'd behave this way. Oh, it wasn't an overt sort of thing. She wasn't coming up and saying nasty things to my face. No, Andie was more subtle about prejudice.

Prejudice?

I froze. Was that what this was about?

After class I stuffed my school books, as well as my library books on personality types, into my locker while Tina waited patiently for me. Being Hispanic, Andie knew full well the pain of racial slurs. It had been fresh on her mind two days ago—the day we watched Ryan Davis, the biggest racist jerk around—from the cafeteria window. Had she forgotten so soon?

My brain clicked off the events of the day. On the one hand, I was leaning toward telling Andie—all the freshmen—the truth about Jeff's father. Jeff Kinney's campaign promise was bogus—there would never be any free soda. It was Jeff's attempt to bribe his way into student council.

Was it fair to let him get by with lying? Besides, what kind of class president would Jeff make if he based his votes on deceit?

On the other hand, the truth could set Andie on the winning track, sail her right through to the victory she longed for. Still, part of me insisted on holding back the secret.

Justice!

20

I kept the news about Jeff's lie quiet through Saturday, which was the fabulous day I *finally* got the kind of haircut I now really wanted. And at an upscale salon this time!

I kept the secret about Jeff and his "soda promise" through most of the whole next week, too.

Things went fairly smoothly. Class quizzes, homework—stuff like that. Tina, however, was the one bump in the road. She kept bringing it up— the "pop" secret. Had I told anyone yet?

Every day she asked me, until I finally set her straight. We were sitting on the school steps waiting for her ride the following Wednesday, the day before campaign speeches were scheduled.

"Why haven't you told anyone?" Tina asked. She sounded fed up. With me. "Andie deserves to know the truth."

"I'm not having this conversation," I said.

Tina's eyelids fluttered. "Why not? What are you waiting for?"

"I have my reasons."

She gasped. "I can't believe you'd let revenge get in the way, Holly. What kind of friend are you?"

I felt like she'd punched me in the stomach. "What?" I whispered.

"You're a Christian, right?"

I wasn't dumb enough to ask how she knew. Christians are supposed to be obvious—stick out in the world. I groaned. "Guess I'm not a very good one."

She was silent. "Well, it's never easy."

I jerked my head to look at her. How did she know, unless . . . "You're a Christian, too."

She smiled. "Since I was nine."

"Wow." I leaned my elbows on my books, thrilled with this news. "So that makes us sisters—in the family of God."

"You're right." Tina seemed pleased to hear me link the two of us as family.

A Ford minivan pulled up to the curb. "I'll call you later, okay?" I held out my arm.

Tina held on to me as we walked down the steps. Before she got in the van, she introduced me to her mother. "Mom, this is Holly Meredith, my new friend. And Holly," Tina continued, turning to me, "this is my mother, Judith Frazer."

"Hello, Holly." The well-groomed, middle-aged woman smiled. "It's lovely to meet you."

"Nice meeting you, too," I said.

I observed the gentle way Tina's mom treated

Tina and Taffy. "Well, are we ready to go?" she asked.

I closed the van door, lingering for a moment. Tina's window slid down. "Don't study too hard," she said.

"Look who's talking."

"Bye, Holly," she called as the van pulled away.

I stood there for the longest time staring after them. Tina had somehow known that I was getting even with Andie by keeping Jeff's secret about the soda. But how? This baffled me totally.

I headed back inside to get my books out of my locker, dragging my feet as I went. The past few days had been rough—I'd stayed up too late doing homework. The lack of sleep was catching up with me.

As I rounded the corner to go to my locker, I stumbled into someone. Looking up, I saw that it was Andie. She was alone—without her usual twin attendants.

"Oh, sorry." I stepped back. "Didn't see you."

"No, it's my fault," she insisted. The light from outside flashed off her new braces.

I turned to go just as I saw Ryan Davis coming toward us. His hands were behind his back and there was a peculiar glint in his eye. "Hey, girls," he called to us.

The hairs on the back of my neck stood up. I sensed something. Impending danger?

Instinct, my mom called it. *"Always pay attention to that sensation,"* she'd warned.

I should've run for it when I had the chance.

Ryan whistled, and out of nowhere came three other guys, all upperclassmen, including Zye Greene. They grabbed me by the arms.

Zye picked up Andie and swung her over his shoulder. "Freshman frenzy!" he hollered gleefully.

"No! No!" Andie yelled. "Put me down!"

"Let me go!" I screamed as they pulled me out the front doors and down the long cement steps toward the flagpole.

"Gorgeous freshmen don't get by without initiation as long as I'm around," Ryan Davis said in my ear.

I wanted to slap him. I pushed and shoved, trying to get free. But I was powerless against the two guys who began tying me to the flagpole.

I could feel them tying Andie up, too.

"You'll be sorry!" she yelled as the boys worked the knots and made them tight. Too tight.

When the deed was done, the despicable upperclassmen fled. I groaned. Here we were, stuck in front of the high school, our arms tied behind a flagpole with clothesline. Holly and Andie—former best friends—tied up together in the worst initiation stunt so far.

"Can you wiggle your hands?" I strained my neck, trying to see Andie behind me.

"Barely," she muttered.

"They must've learned some super-holding boy scout knots or something," I wailed.

"You're right." She was kicking and thrashing around as though her life depended on it.

I heard the city bus blow out puffs of exhaust

as it made the turn away from the school. "There goes my ride!"

Andie moaned. "Mine, too. That's why I was rushing and nearly ran into you before." Her voice cracked with desperation. "This is humiliating . . . and disgusting."

"And the worst of it is, tomorrow's the day we cast our votes for student council."

"What?" She began to laugh. That mid-range laugh with an eerie staccato bounce. "Here we are, tied to a flagpole, and you're talking about ballot boxes? C'mon, Holly, you've got to be kidding."

I thought about what she'd just said. About other things, too. The way she'd booted me out of her cozy campaign hoopla. The frivolous phone comments she'd made over the past week—and hanging up on me . . .

"We're not very good friends anymore, are we?" I said.

"Well, it's not my fault."

"Look, Andie. I'm not pointing fingers. It's just that . . . well, we used to share our secrets. All of them."

"Secrets are childish," she said. "Face it, we're growing up, past the stage of Loyalty Papers and best friends and all that dumb stuff. It's better to have lots of friends; at least for me it is."

All that dumb stuff . . .

Her words stung me. What Andie was saying fit right into what Mom had told me about extroverts. When they grew up, they required lots of friends. Not just one.

I stuck my neck out and came close to confiding in her. "I'm trying to branch out, make new friends," I managed to say. "But it's not as easy for people like me."

"Are we talking about Tina now?" She sounded more hesitant than brash.

"Blind isn't bad, you know."

"Who said it was?"

"Well, the way you and the Miller twins acted," I said, not really wanting to bring it up, "well, I was actually glad Tina couldn't see the three of you."

Andie sighed. "You probably won't believe this, but I really felt lousy about it later. I mean, it hasn't been so long ago—remember last summer and the low-down comments Ryan Davis made about me? I know how it feels to be treated poorly when you're . . . uh . . . different."

She was backpedaling. "Forgive me, Holly?" she said.

"Always." And I meant it.

Suddenly Andie began to cry. Soft, whimpering sounds. "My hands feel really numb," she said. "I'm scared we're stuck here all night."

"Maybe we should stop trying to loosen the cord. Maybe the guys made knots that get tighter when you struggle." I wiggled my fingers. "I'm not sure, but I think my fingers are tingling. They feel really weird."

"Oh, Holly," Andie cried, "what if the blood circulation goes out of our hands? What if our hands have to be amputated?"

"There goes my writing career," I moaned, joining her in the drama.

"And what about me? I'm the accompanist for show choir this year."

"C'mon, Andie. Get a grip. We have to relax." I felt overwhelmed. "Maybe if we yell, the janitor or the principal will hear us."

"Good idea." And she started hollering at the top of her lungs. So did I.

I'd never seen Andie so freaked. Usually she was the calm one under stress.

When we were exhausted from yelling, I suggested that we pray. "I'll start."

Andie agreed. "Why didn't we think of this first?"

"Dear Lord," I began, "please send someone to help us so we won't have to spend the night out here."

"Amen to someone finding us," she prayed.

We quieted down somewhat, although Andie was still moaning. At last I began to talk. "I've been holding out on you about something, Andie. I need to tell you the truth about Jeff Kinney."

"What truth?"

There was no way out now. I had to tell her. Maybe this initiation was supposed to happen to us. Maybe we were supposed to get strung up to the flagpole.

Together.

21

"*So are you going to tell me or not?*" Andie demanded.

I struggled with my fabulous secret.

"Holly?"

"All right, I'll tell you," I said. "Tina overheard something last week." I paused, thinking how this moment could possibly change the course of the entire school year. Possibly the course of Andie's and my future relationship. "Tina heard Mark Jones telling some girl about Jeff's dad," I continued.

"Whoa! Slow down," Andie insisted. "I don't get what you're saying."

I repeated the circumstances again. Slowly. Then I revealed the truth. "Jeff's dad is not a soda-pop dealer."

"Huh?"

"His dad is a doctor, for pete's sake."

"Are you sure?"

"Isn't it obvious? I mean, if he's a doctor, he's not a pop dealer."

She fidgeted. "What if he's both?"

I hadn't thought of that. "I think we should call Mr. Kinney and check things out."

"Tonight?" she said, out of breath.

"As soon as someone frees us from this flagpole nightmare."

She yelled some more. Louder this time.

"Let's yell 'fire,' " I suggested. "People pay attention to that."

"Hey, you're right."

So we yelled "Fire! Fire!" until we were hoarse.

Finally Mr. Crane and two other teachers poked their heads out a window. "Where's the fire?" the principal called to us. He was serious.

"Right here," Andie shouted. "I've got rope burns on my wrists." Andie was in rare form.

After the principal left the window, I said to Andie, "Looks like we survived part of freshman initiation, or whatever Zye Greene called it."

"Freshman frenzy," Andie grunted.

"Well, if this is all there is to it—"

"Don't be too sure," Andie scoffed. "Knowing Zye and Ryan, there's probably more to come."

"I hope not. I've had my share."

Mr. Crane came with a scissors and cut us free. "Are you girls all right?" He looked concerned. "Who did this to you?"

"We'd better not say," Andie spoke up. "Seniors hate freshmen, you know."

"Thanks for rescuing us," I said. "We were getting worried there for a while."

"I can see that," he said, eyeing Andie's wrists. "You'd better soak your wrists in Epsom salts when you get home."

She nodded. "We need to make a phone call first."

"That's fine; follow me." And the two of us hurried into the building and gathered up Andie's books and things, which were still strewn around the hallway.

I borrowed the office phone book and located the number for Jeff Kinney's father. Sure enough— Edward Kinney, M.D.

Andie was still rubbing her wrists when I dialed the phone. "What're you going to say?" she whispered.

"Just listen to the pro."

The receptionist sounded pleasant enough. "Doctor Kinney's office."

"Hello, I'm a friend of Jeff Kinney," I said. "Is this his father's office?"

"Yes."

"Well, I was wondering if I could check on something."

"Certainly. How may I help you?"

I took a deep breath, hoping this wouldn't sound too ridiculous. "Jeff's telling everyone at school that his dad's a soda dealer, but you just said this is a doctor's office."

"That's right."

"Then are you saying Dr. Kinney won't be bringing free soft drinks to school every Friday for the rest of the school year?"

The receptionist began to laugh. "Well, I think I'd be one of the first to know about it, since I'm Dr. Kinney's wife—Jeff's mom."

I explained about the campaign promises. "I guess Jeff really wants to be class president this year."

"Class president?" she echoed.

"Didn't you know?"

She wasn't laughing now. "I will definitely talk to Jeff tonight. And what did you say your name was, hon?"

"I didn't say." And I hung up.

Andie was about to burst. "You're too cool, Holly. Wait'll I tell everyone about this."

"Hey, you'll win tomorrow—no problem." Part of me still missed the old Andie. The old us. But most of all, I missed the secret. The secret that might've saved us—kept Andie all for myself. Kept her from being linked up with the student council clique.

Andie beamed. "How can I ever thank you?" I thought she was going to hug me, but she didn't. Her smile said it all. "Well, we better get going. It's a long walk home."

We walked together for three blocks. Andie did most of the talking. She was wired up about the prospect of her position on the student council.

Me? I was having a hard time not dwelling on the past. Our past—Andie's and mine. But Mom's words echoed in my brain. "*Sometimes people drift apart during high school . . ."*

"So, where do you see yourself in ten years?" I asked.

She didn't waste a second responding. "Hopefully, married to a terrific Christian guy. Someone who wants a big family."

I should've known. "And what about all the experience you'll get on the student council? How will that fit into your life?"

"Hey, I didn't agree to an interview yet. Wait till I get voted in." She giggled gleefully. "Oh . . . about student council. I'll definitely use my experience later in life. I want lots of kids, remember? And right here in Dressel Hills."

I nodded.

Andie continued. "Being class president means you have to learn to delegate power—you know, assign jobs. My high-school experience will fit right in with my future; you can bet on that."

I smiled. Andie was so sure of herself. I liked that.

"What about friends? When you get super popular, will you remember who your first friends were?"

Andie grabbed my arm. "I'll never forget you, Holly. Never."

I grinned. "Just remember who got you elected freshman class president."

"Don't worry," she said as we headed in different directions. I hoped it was just a short parting of the ways. Maybe, in time, we'd have our close bond again. Maybe not. Either way, I had fabulous memories . . . and hope for the future. And a widening circle of friends. Sort of.

After supper I made at least twenty phone calls, getting the word out about Jeff Kinney—and no free soda! Everyone I talked to promised to vote for Andie.

Later, I called Tina. "Got any plans this weekend?"

"Not really. Why?"

"How would you like to have supper at my house Friday?"

"I'd love to," she said. "But let me ask Mom first."

When she came back, she said it was fine.

"Great. Maybe we can write some poetry together," I suggested.

"Or we could read some of our stories to each other," she said, referring to her Braille machine.

"Good idea." Tina didn't know I had zillions of notebooks full of stories and poems and things. Thoughts about life, generally and specifically. Shoot, this girl probably didn't know what she was getting herself into.

"I heard you got initiated today," she said.

"So did Andie. We were tied to the flagpole."

"Together?"

"It was bizarre at first, but then she and I started talking. We talked a lot. And I told her about Jeff."

"It's about time."

"I know." I felt ashamed again.

"Glad you did, Holly. I was praying for you."

I wasn't used to hearing that a friend was praying. Well, except for Danny Myers.

"I'd better get going," Tina said. "See you tomorrow."

"No, you won't," I teased. "You'll smell me tomorrow. Better watch out—I might be wearing different perfume."

"Hey, you wouldn't do that to me, would you?" With that, we burst into giggles and hung up.

After my homework was done, I made two very cool posters to wave during tomorrow's assembly. One for Tina, and one for me.

22

The next morning while I waited for Carrie to get out of the bathroom (she was taking longer than ever these days!), I wrote in my journal.

Thursday, September 19: Today Andie gives her campaign speech. She's first, then Jeff Kinney. I can't wait to see what he does when I hold up my poster. It says: No Friday Pop—Jeff's Pop's a Doc!

Everyone knows by now that Jeff lied about having free soda at school. Thanks to all the phone calls Andie and I made last night. The way I see it, she's destined for class president. Jared and Amy-Liz will probably make it, too. They've been campaigning like crazy. And Billy's going to be a great class treasurer if he gets elected.

Sometimes I wish I had run for office. But then I think about Tina. When it comes right down to it, I know I'd rather be helping her than getting frazzled over school politics and stuff. Besides, I really like her.

After "losing" Andie to the student council thing,

*I never dreamed my heart could accept someone new
as a close friend . . . and so fast. Yesterday Andie said
she'd never forget me. Well, I won't hold her to it,
because I can see her changing. And with change
comes the growing apart process—the toughest part of
all. Maybe I shouldn't blame it on Andie. Maybe I'm
changing, too. . . .*

♥ ♥ ♥

After a bunch of homeroom preliminaries, we
headed to the assembly. I sat with Tina one row
behind Billy Hill and his fans. Tina got her guide
dog situated directly under her seat for the half-
hour session.

"I'll tell you when to hold up your poster," I
said.

Her face shone. "This is so exciting!"

"I know." But I had a fleeting thought—a
lonely, sentimental feeling—floating around in my
brain. And when I scanned the audience for
Andie, I noticed she was sitting in the front row
with Amy-Liz and Jared. Any other time I
would've been there beside her. Encouraging her.
Saying all the right words.

I refused to think about what used to be and
turned my attention to Tina. Something intrigued
me about her. Maybe it was her positive, upbeat
approach to life. She was blind, yet she seemed so
happy.

Just then Mr. Crane was onstage, standing at the podium. The students got quiet. Anticipation, like electricity, crackled in the air. "We have student business to conduct today." The crowd broke into wild applause.

When things settled down again, the principal continued with his introductions.

At last Andie stood in front of us. She wore her new outfit. I listened intently to her opening remarks. Honestly, I couldn't remember ever seeing her in a position of leadership like this. I wracked my brain trying to recall a time . . .

Then I heard my name!

"At this time, I would like to thank Holly Meredith for her support and encouragement. Tina Frazer, in her own special way, was a great help, too. Several sophomore friends of mine, including Paula and Kayla Miller, were responsible for running my campaign. . . ."

The fact that she'd mentioned my name—and first, before the twins—soothed my sore heart.

"I will not make promises that I cannot keep," Andie was saying. "The thing I will do, however, is lead my class to the best of my ability. And with your help—each of you in this room—I will represent your needs, listen to your problems, and do my best to come up with solutions. Thank you for your vote of confidence—I'll see you at the polls!"

Wow, I was impressed. Andie's speech didn't sound anything like what the Miller twins might've written. And the more I thought about it, I knew Andie hadn't written it, either.

"Great speech," I said to Tina who was also on her feet clapping.

"Not bad for a first timer?" she said, with a strange smile on her face.

I had no idea what she meant. "First timer?"

"Your friend called me last night and offered me ten bucks to write her speech," Tina said. "It was easier than I thought."

"Andie hired you to write it?" I shouldn't have been surprised. Andie was unpredictable. That part of her hadn't changed one bit.

Andie walked down the steps, heading confidently toward her seat. Just once, I wished she'd glance up and see me clapping for her, cheering for her. . . .

We took our seats and waited to hear Jeff Kinney's speech. I couldn't imagine that he hadn't heard what we'd been spreading around about him. Bottom line: He was not an honest guy.

"Hold up your poster," I whispered to Tina.

Lots of other students were waving gimmicky posters as Jeff Kinney approached the stage, shuffling his papers.

The auditorium was still. Jeff stood at the podium and coughed. I felt embarrassed for him, wondering what he could possibly say to save face. "Fellow classmates, teachers, and Mr. Crane," he began.

Oh, brother, he's pouring it on, I thought.

"Today I stand before you to stand behind you, to tell you something I know nothing about."

Snickering rippled through the audience.

"Now . . . to get things straight right from here on out," he continued, "my dad's not going to be able to supply free soda on Fridays as previously promised. He will, however, offer free flu shots to any student this winter. Thanks for your support."

By now, Jeff's face had turned a bright red. And as he made his way off the stage, only a few of his close friends applauded. It was an awkward moment for everyone, and I touched Tina's elbow and told her to put her poster away.

We listened to the other candidates' speeches, and at the end I decided that Andie's was best. "It was perfect," I told Tina. "You wrote a fabulous campaign speech."

"Thanks," she said, leaning over to whisper to her guide dog. I carried both the posters as we headed up the aisle, toward the hallway doors.

During lunch, Tina and I went to study hall where the ballot boxes were set up. I helped her find the square she wanted to check. When she was finished, I waited for her to fold her ballot. Carefully, she felt for the opening on the ballot box and dropped the paper in.

♥ ♥ ♥

I had an email message from Sean when I arrived home. I couldn't wait to read it.

Hey, Holly,
*   Well, how do you feel about writing to a bald guy?*

Seriously, I did it. I shaved my head! Most all the guys in Mr. Fremont's class did, too. It's weird what some people will do to encourage a friend.

I thought about Sean's words. And I thought about Andie. I hadn't shaved my head or anything drastic, but I had done something. Something to assure her a desired goal.

Mom had said flexibility was a big part of growing up. Was that happening? Was I growing up?

I stared at the computer screen. Sean was a perfect example of true maturity. I couldn't wait to write him back, so I clicked on Reply and began typing away.

23

The next morning Mr. Crane's voice came over the intercom with election results. "Andrea Martinez has been voted in as president of the freshman class, Jared Wilkins was elected vice-president, Amy-Liz Thompson will be the new secretary for the class, and Billy Hill is the treasurer. Congratulations to each of these fine students."

The hall at lunchtime was crowded with well-wishers, streamers, balloons, and confetti. I hurried to pick up Tina and Taffy in study hall, then we made our way through the tangle of humanity.

"Do you mind if we stop by Andie's locker?" I asked Tina.

"No problem," she said, reminding me of Andie.

I laughed, but I was sure she didn't hear me. Not against the backdrop of hilarious celebration. When we found Andie, she was being swarmed by half the freshman class. At least, that's how it appeared as I waited with Tina for a chance to congratulate the winner.

Even Stan showed his face, in spite of his sophomore status. And when he walked past me, he gave me a decent smile for a change.

Andie sparkled as she talked to her adoring fans, hugging them, thanking them, and accepting their enthusiastic remarks. And from my vantage point, I surprised myself by not feeling so left out.

I was actually part of it all. I'd helped make this moment happen for Andie, and I was glad.

Nobody could move, it was so crowded. But I waited patiently, and then it happened. Andie glanced up, and her eyes caught mine. "Holly! Holly-Heart, get yourself over here," she called.

"C'mon," I said to Tina, guiding her to Andie. The mass of devotees parted like the Red Sea as we came. Then Andie hugged me hard.

"You did it, girl," I said. "Congratulations!"

"*We* did it," Andie said, not letting go of me. "Thanks for everything." I knew what she meant. So did Tina. And long after the throng of kids had gone, Andie, Tina, and I hung around talking.

When the Miller twins finally caught up with the three of us, we were sitting in the cafeteria, well within the seniors' silly boundary line.

"Congrats," Paula said.

"We heard the news," Kayla said.

"Isn't she fabulous?" I said about Andie.

The twins agreed. Tina, too. We sat there reliving the events of the past two days, and I never once felt a twinge of pain. Sure, my circle of friends had begun to widen, but the Holly-Andie bond was as strong as ever. The only difference was it didn't encompass every inch of our lives. It didn't have to.

We were freshmen now, for pete's sake.

About the Author

Beverly Lewis clearly remembers her freshman year in high school—she shared a locker with a girl who turned out to be a Christian, too. She also remembers the pain of losing a close friend to another girl. She recorded the incident in her secret diary. Eventually her circle of friends widened again to replace the loss.

Many fans have written to tell Beverly about their problems with relationships. "Growing up can be tough sometimes," she says, "but things are easier—and sweeter—when you have a friend like Jesus."

Beverly still answers all her email with a personal response. Contact her via her Web site at *www.BeverlyLewis.com*.

Also by Beverly Lewis

PICTURE BOOKS

Cows in the House   Annika's Secret Wish
Just Like Mama

THE CUL-DE-SAC KIDS
Children's Fiction

The Double Dabble Surprise   Tarantula Toes
The Chicken Pox Panic   Green Gravy
The Crazy Christmas Angel Mystery   Backyard Bandit Mystery
No Grown-ups Allowed   Tree House Trouble
Frog Power   The Creepy Sleep-Over
The Mystery of Case D. Luc   The Great TV Turn-Off
The Stinky Sneakers Mystery   Piggy Party
Pickle Pizza   The Granny Game
Mailbox Mania   Mystery Mutt
The Mudhole Mystery   Big Bad Beans
Fiddlesticks   The Upside-Down Day
The Crabby Cat Caper   The Midnight Mystery

ABRAM'S DAUGHTERS
Adult Fiction

The Covenant

THE HERITAGE OF LANCASTER COUNTY
Adult Fiction

The Shunning   The Confession
The Reckoning

OTHER ADULT FICTION

The Postcard
The Crossroad

The Redemption of Sarah Cain

October Song

Sanctuary*

The Sunroom

www.BeverlyLewis.com

*with David Lewis

PUT YOUR LIFE ON THE RIGHT PATH

Bible Studies Written Just for Teens!

Kevin Johnson's TEEN DISCIPLESHIP series is a unique series written just for you. Pointing you toward a vital, heart-to-heart, sold-out relationship with God, each book tackles an important topic like prayer, understanding the Bible, choosing friends, and much more.

1. Get God
2. Wise Up
3. Cross Train
4. Pray Hard
5. See Jesus
6. Stick Tight
7. Get Smart
8. Bust Loose